P9-DNE-057

The Secret
of the
Ballet Book

The Secret
of the
Ballet Book

Navita Dello

Copyright © 2015 Navita Dello
All rights reserved worldwide. No part of this publication may be
reproduced, stored in a retrieval system or transmitted in any form
or by any means, electronic or otherwise, without written
permission from the author.

The moral right of the author has been asserted.

ISBN 978-0-9943509-1-6

Cover design by Tatiana Vila

This book is written in Australian English.

*In memory of my grandparents,
my childhood gems*

Chapter 1

Sierra shuddered at the verdict. How could she quit the only thing she wanted to do? The one thing she hadn't changed her mind about for a whole six years, the thing she had even set out in a three-step plan?

She'd die if she had to; just die.

That's why she had to find that book she'd browsed through a few days ago – it could be what might save her from having to quit. *She would not leave Reads without it!*

But it wasn't where she had spotted it before.

It wasn't on the lower shelves.

It wasn't *anywhere.*

She dumped the nagging thought that it might have been sold; she couldn't let that distract her. Purple: she was certain it had a purplish cover. She craned her neck and scanned the rows that towered over her, mumbling, '*The Ballerina's Treasure Trove,*' as if the book would hear her call its name.

Where was it?

Sierra glared at the well-stocked shelves. Had it been whisked from Performing Arts and chucked elsewhere? Was that permitted?

A hand shot past her nose and shoved a book onto a shelf.

It had a violet jacket.

It seemed the right size …

Her pulse thudded. She leaned in and peered at the spine.

The Ballerina's Treasure Trove.

Sierra plucked the book from the shelf. Her heart did a dance of gallops and hops. Quickly, she flipped to the pages she'd noticed earlier. Yay. A treasure trove of sequences that linked the steps she'd done in class. Relieved, she let out a puff of air. Even Miss Lana would have to agree that these combinations could lift her dancing. *Surely*, they'd land her with the role of Princess Aurora – and bring her mum to her senses.

Give up ballet for schoolwork? Seriously.

Sierra unglued her gaze from the book and closed it reluctantly. Somewhere, she'd read that Anna Pavlova's inspiration to attend ballet classes came from seeing a performance of *The Sleeping Beauty*. So winding up as the star in that show could be just the way to *inspire* her mum to back off about ballet.

Sierra's yelling hadn't done it.

Her pleading hadn't done it.

Her crying hadn't done it.

She cradled the book. *This* had to. How could a famous-ballerina-to-be drop out of ballet school?

Whoops, her ballet class. Was she late? Sierra checked her watch and then ducked past the customers along the narrow aisle of the second-hand bookshop, her mum's voice chugging in her head. 'You're a scholarship winner!' she had exploded, as if Sierra didn't know that. But it had been all that *stuff* in her eyes when she spoke which made something inside Sierra snap.

At the cash register, she caught sight of Min. Though it would have stoked her usually, she muttered, 'Oh, no.' Suppose Min guessed she was gearing for the audition with this book and told the others at the dance centre? So not cool; she had to avoid her.

Min, however, was already peeking from under her fringe. 'Hiya,' she said. 'What have you got ...? *The Ballerina's Treasure –*'

'We'll be late for our class,' Sierra said.

8

'You are getting edgy!' Min flashed her an understanding grin. 'Okay, fine, go before me. I realise Saturday afternoon is the best part of your week. And I can handle Miss Lana's punctuality-is-rule-number-one-at-the-Lana-Lott-Dance-Centre look.'

'Thanks,' Sierra said, and swapped places with her in the queue. Then she ignored the flutter in her heart and let Min thumb through the book because she was always a good sport.

When Sierra got to the front of the line, Mrs Vickers scraped back some silvery ringlets that had strayed from their rightful position in her crop of hair and smiled at the book. 'A good one,' she said, and keyed in the details. 'Fan of ballet?'

Sierra piled nine dollars and ninety-five cents on the counter.

She swallowed.

'I'm going to be a ballerina,' she replied.

∞

When Sierra got home after ballet, she dashed up to her room and laid *The Ballerina's Treasure Trove* gently on the empty side of her desk.

Entries first. She dug into her private-collections drawer for her ballet journal, drew a tissue from the box beside her and wiped the black hard cover till it shone. She'd chosen black because it was classic, like ballet. Then she picked the sleek pen she'd begged from her dad, as it appeared fit for writing about anything *classic*, and flicked to her last note. Now for today.

She couldn't wait to record Miss Lana's praises.

'*Pas de chat*: nice', she scrawled in her tall slanted letters. 'Mew, mew.' She had to be jumping like a cat because getting a compliment from Miss Lana wasn't easy. In brackets she inserted, 'Think *cat*'.

'*Balancé*: lovely', she penned in, next. 'Ah-ha!' A notch higher than the *nice* she'd got last time. The *Lana* tip on moving to the waltz in this step had worked. Within brackets she made another note: 'Think *one-two-three, one-two-three ...*'

Sierra reclined in her chair and coiled her short hair behind her ears. Listing Miss Lana's remarks was handy for tracking progress and deciding what to practise. She stole a glance at *The Ballerina's Treasure Trove* and then toyed with her pen because she had to jot down Miss Lana's corrections.

Instead, she found herself leafing through her previous entries in the journal. Soon, she heard a sigh escape her lips and shook her head from side to side. These *lovelies* weren't enough to turn her into Princess Aurora, not with Miss Lana hunting like a hawk for perfection. She'd have to get *perfects*. Pages of them.

She reached for the ballet book. 'Hmm ...' She'd already fathomed she had to practise. Lots. But now it was clear that her dancing needed more lifting than she'd expected. A formal training program, yup, the *real deal* – that's what she had to come up with. That was task one.

Sierra sprang out of her chair with the book and sank cross-legged into the greenish twists on her squiggly rug. Why couldn't people be allowed to keep their dreams?

Here she was to audition to preserve that career she had mapped, that three-step plan. From the *corps de ballet*, the main group, in one of those neat dance troupes she'd seen on television when she was five ... to the soloist she'd wanted to be once she put on her first pair of ballet shoes ... to the prima ballerina she believed she could become after having her first ballet class.

Her lower lip trembled at the fear of losing it all. How was she going to be perfect by the end of this term?

Sierra bit her lip to stop the trembling and raised her eyes to the clock on her bedside table. Was it being noisy or was that tick in her head? She dived into the ballet book. In a while, her shrivelled spirits bloomed.

'Princess Aurora!' She beamed at the page-sized picture of a dancer posing with one arm gracefully stretched in front of her, and the other arm and a leg lifted behind her. 'A perfect *arabesque*,' she said, as though she were Miss Lana. She placed *The Ballerina's Treasure Trove* on the rug and bent over to study it further.

But ...

The picture was blurring.

Frowning, she stared.

Then blinked.

It was shaking ...

How weird! Sierra let out a startled grunt and slithered backwards away from the book. Could a picture quiver?

Chapter 2

Sierra squeezed her eyes shut. The flickering darkness now behind her lids wasn't as creepy as being tricked by a picture. But what if the quivering did happen? Was happening still? Terrified by that thought, she opened her eyes a trifle, yet it wasn't enough to see. She slid up to the book again, lifting her eyelids little by little till she was peering at the page.

The picture *was* trembling ...

Losing vigour ...

Becoming a shadow ...

Getting darker ...

Ah? The shadow had formed into the shape of a person.

A movement!

Sierra jerked, raising her head from the page.

A bit.

She gripped the rug, her eyes widening.

Standing in third position wearing pink satin ballet shoes was a pair of feet.

She lifted her head a bit more.

Her mouth opened.

Those feet belonged to legs in silky tights.

Now bit by bit she raised her head past knees which were turned out sideways until her eyes met layers and layers of net that swished in her ears. They seemed as though they were from the blue-green tutu in the –

Sierra fell back, digging her elbows into the rug.

The ballerina in the picture.

Unreal! A dream! Ooooor? She scrambled to her feet. Then a rap on the door almost booted her out of her skin.

'Sierra?'

Sierra's blood curdled. 'Hang on, Mum!' Panic surging inside her, she stared at the dancer.

The ballerina pointed her finger at the book.

Was she real?

'Close the book,' she said in a soft voice. 'Quick!'

Sierra saw the door knob turn. She gasped, leapt forward and kicked the book shut.

Whoosh! Gone, without a trace.

In the nick of time too for Sierra's mum's gaze was roaming the room. 'You look as if you've seen an alien from beyond,' she said. 'And thought I heard somebody!'

'Me, Mum, learning a poem for Monday,' Sierra said, trying her best to sound casual in spite of the zillion question marks pricking her brain.

Her mum draped her arms round Sierra's shoulders, only to snatch them away. 'Sweetie, you're shivering, and you're wet. Feel sick?'

Sierra groaned at her mum's worry-worry routine. Seriously, why this evening? Why this hour? Why this minute? Once she got started ... With a desperate glance at the ballet book, Sierra clamped her teeth and allowed the hand-on-the-forehead, the do-you-have-fever thing.

'We'd better pop into the Coomb Street Medical Centre,' her mum concluded. 'See the –'

'But, Mum, I'm fine. I was practising my moves before doing the poem, that's why I'm sweaty.' Sierra invented a few more reasons for being perfectly well, while in her head the ballerina was doing a scene from Princess Aurora's sixteenth birthday. She *had* to get to the book. 'If I have even a sniffle in the morning, I'll go to the doctor,' she said.

Her mum looked her up and down as though she was expecting to spot symptoms of whatever she suspected was the case. 'Well ... I suppose,' she said, and stepped back, nearly tripping on *The Ballerina's Treasure Trove*. With a swoop she beat Sierra to it.

Then she opened the book.

'Mum, no!' Her heart booming, Sierra grabbed it and then at her mum's taken aback expression, conjured a laugh. 'Er ... I want to give you a demo when I'm done,' she said, chiding herself for her lame excuse.

Her mum rolled her eyes. 'Umm ... What have you got in there?'

'Exercises! New ones to practise, for the audition.'

'You won't have time for ballet with your schoolwork,' her mum said. 'We discussed this yesterday.'

'I know, Mum, I know! But you said I could do the end-of-term audition and take part in the concert which is *next* term.'

'And only till then.' Her mum's voice was coated with clarity – her mind was made up.

Sierra's stomach rumbled.

'Came to tell you about Grandma,' her mum went on, 'but that'll have to wait or else dinner will be late.'

With a click of the door she was gone.

On the rug in a jiffy, Sierra tossed the pages. Where was the ballerina? Or maybe she *was* ill, raging with a fever that was making her see things. 'Think, think, Sierra,' she said, and that propelled her to the contents. Then she ran her finger through the headings and got to the section she sought.

Fantasy: Fairy Tales

She kept going down.

Cinderella

Little Red Riding Hood

The Sleeping Beauty

Her hands tingling, she fumbled to get to page 27 – the start of *The Sleeping Beauty*. She flipped to the next page, the next and the next.

She was ogling at Princess Aurora.

It was page 33.

And, again, the picture was fluttering.

Sierra struggled to her feet on wobbly knees.

The shadow! The shadow! It was shaping into that human figure she'd seen earlier, sort of marking the place of the dancer who was stepping out of the page ...

Sierra edged back although itching to reach over and tap her to test whether she was real.

Now the ballerina was smiling with a sparkle that matched her diamond tiara, and also her eyes, oh, like aquamarines were shinier than the sequins on her blue-green tutu. 'Lucky me!' she said. 'Out twice in one day.'

Sierra moved her jaws, but the words got stuck in her throat.

The dancer didn't appear to notice the silence because she was gazing round the room. 'Lovely to be here,' she said. Then on her toes she spun with her arms in fifth position, a neat oval above her head.

Sierra tried not to blink.

Soon the ballerina dropped lightly to her feet. 'I'm Rosella ... but Princess Aurora in the picture. I heard your mum say "Sierra" when she knocked.'

Sierra couldn't help gawking. Why was she acting *normal*? Why didn't she discharge rays of light from her body that would illuminate the air around her, or something, to reveal she was mythical? When none of that happened, Sierra coughed out the words still clinging to her throat. 'How? What?'

'Oh, Sierra, it's a painful story ... a very painful story.' Gone was the glow in Rosella's eyes. They were so misty that Sierra couldn't catch their colour which, minutes ago, had seemed blue-green like the dancer's tutu.

'You see,' Rosella said, 'my neighbour Azra despised dancing. She hated it. *Revolting* she called it to see me doing ballet whenever she peeped through her window. She demanded I end it, but I had to practise.'

'And?'

'I didn't know, of course, that she was a witch –'

'A *witch*?' A chill pattered along Sierra's spine.

'And to get rid of me, that witch trapped me in this book.'

'But how?'

'With magic spells.'

The chill loitering in Sierra's spine scrolled up her neck and entered her head. '*Spells?*'

Rosella nodded. 'Azra told me that although she usually didn't cast spells in the neighbourhood to avoid attracting attention, she was going to treat me as an exception ... because I had disregarded her warning. So she cast a *live-in* spell naming page 33 as the page she was going to stick me in, and then a *no-way-out* spell, chanting all the other page numbers to prevent me from getting away through those pages. But ...' Rosella lifted her index finger. 'She forgot to mention page 33 again. Therefore the *no-way-out* spell doesn't apply to that page. It had to be her fury that led to her mistake.'

'Ah!' Sierra said. 'Explains why you can come out of the book when it's turned to page 33.'

'You got it!'

'And, is closing the book the only way to put you back on the page?'

'Precisely!'

'Let's tear the book,' Sierra said. 'It can't draw you into it then. Ever!'

'*Tear it?*' Rosella's pinkish complexion was marred with horror.

'What I meant,' Sierra said, baffled by her reaction, 'was that no one can shut the book if we shred it.'

Rosella's lips curved down to her chin.

Sierra pursed hers; she had to keep her big mouth in check. She was upsetting Rosella for some reason.

'Not that simple,' Rosella said quietly. 'Before Azra returned the book to the shop she got it from, she also cast another spell to make certain I remained trapped – tied to the book.'

'T-tied? How?'

'Urm, well, because of that spell –'

'Yup?'

'Even if I made it out of the book, as I have now, I must re-enter the page within two hours. Otherwise –'

'*Yup?*'

'I will disappear!'

'*Whaaaaaat?*' Sierra wrapped her arms round Rosella's slender waist as if to save her from drifting into the air.

'So you see? We can't destroy the book.'

Sierra's brain pumped in her head, digesting everything Rosella had said. She clasped her hands and raised them to her chest miming a *promise*. 'I *won't* let you disappear. I won't!'

'Whenever I'm out,' Rosella said, with two fingers held up, 'remember to close the book within the two-hour deadline to let me in.'

'Will do,' Sierra said, with her eyes peeled to Rosella. 'You must be going cranky missing your family and everything.' In her mind, she spent a busy second telling her own family, Rory too, that they were forgiven, without the tiniest grudge, for wrongdoings they had bestowed upon her for the last eleven years. Apart from the ballet issue, she tagged on immediately. 'First, we must contact your people,' she then said.

Rosella was speechless for what felt like a day and a half. 'I don't have a family,' she said at last. 'My parents died in a car crash. It was rotten. Didn't believe there was more to come. Wrong, wasn't I?'

'Oh, no.'

'After that I lived with my aunt in her little blue cottage. Stayed on even once I grew up because Aunt Helen was ailing by then, and couldn't manage on her own.' Rosella gaped at the calendar on Sierra's desk. 'Oh, my! That was years ago. Aunt Helen won't be there now.'

'But, but you can't be more than about er ... twenty?' Sierra asked.

'Well, I was eighteen when Azra got me. Why I've remained that age is because I'm in this book – time stands still for me when I'm inside.' Rosella shook her hand vigorously. 'I can never go back as that witch will be around. She said she had a *forever* life, meaning she would never die!'

A flood of despair ravaged Sierra again. She had to put a stop to this ... this nightmare. 'Then let's get the spells broken,' she said.

Rosella's face crumpled. 'Azra told me that nobody else can break those spells because they're the worst of the worst. *Ex*-something-or-the-other she called them. And it's not only that!'

'Wh-what do you mean?'

'She even said she'd track me down and make me disappear if I found a way to live out of the book *permanently*. See? Trying to escape is useless! Dangerous!'

All seemed lost.

Sierra drowned in hopelessness despite sensing Rosella rising above it. Rosella appeared to have derived her own dismal reality, and wasn't going to meddle with what she couldn't change and get sucked into what could be worse, like turning into vapour ... a puddle ... a heap ... Sierra shut her mind. Thinking of the *disappearing* act was giving her a headache that wasn't disappearing.

'Then what are we going to *do*?' she cried.

'Nothing,' Rosella said gently.

Sierra gulped, imagining others fleeing from this cruel, hideous set-up by toppling buildings or mountains or anything else that got in their way. But maybe, just maybe, Rosella was wise like the Lilac Fairy in *The Sleeping Beauty,* she thought. The Fairy of Wisdom, after all, didn't lose heart because she couldn't break the evil fairy Carabosse's curse to make Princess Aurora die. She did what she could by willing the princess to sleep, instead – and didn't that work well?

Rosella was at her side now patting her shoulder. 'Thank you, Sierra, thank you for caring. It's been a long time since anyone has. And here you are being kind to a stranger. With that generous heart, you have to be *special.* Tell me about yourself.'

Sierra heard the end-of-the-story tone in her voice; plainly, she didn't want to speak of herself any longer. Then as the fuzz in Sierra's head cleared, Rosella's composure rubbed off on her. She stood with her heels together and feet turned out to the sides in first position. 'My dream is to become a dancer,' she said.

Rosella gave her another radiant smile. 'Sierra Ballerina!'

Sierra pirouetted in her mind.

'Wonderful, might I say. You've got to be keen, buying this ballet book. And, aren't I glad you did? See, this way, I get to dance.' She did an *arabesque*; it looked even more graceful than in the picture on page 33.

Watching Rosella lower her back leg daintily, Sierra clapped with her fingers. 'Guess what? I might also get to be Princess Aurora. My ballet school is performing *The Sleeping Beauty* for their junior concert, and I'm auditioning for a solo.'

'That's splendid,' Rosella said in that soft voice of hers.

In fact, everything about Rosella reminded Sierra of silk, rose petals, butterflies, marshmallows ... Freaky, she thought, how someone so brave could be delicately masked.

Rosella tilted her head and regarded Sierra. 'Charming,' she said. 'A Princess Aurora with crystal blue eyes, sandy brown hair and ...' In a whisper she added, 'Deep, long dimples ... Perhaps –'

Then with a word playing on her lips she was jolted by the drumming on the door.

Chapter 3

Sierra snapped the book shut and slid it under her bed in a trice. Rory. Who else would sound like the Rhythms of Africa show they'd been to? And he never waited for an invitation.

She was right.

The door flung open and her brother stood there with his hands on his hips. 'Dinner!' he bellowed. 'Didn't you hear Mum?' He pasted a stupid grin on his face.

'Oh-oh,' Sierra mumbled.

'Or were you doing the soppy-soppy?' He raised a leg in front of him and waved his arms around.

Same old, same old. Sierra ignored his grin as well as his dance act. He wasn't going to cut out teasing her about ballet. Not ever. How could that tot she used to call Ro-Boy evolve into this six-year-old pest? Knowing he wouldn't budge until she did, she stalked from the room. *Arrrggghhh!* What had Rosella tried to say?

∞

Although dinner had dragged on, back in her room Sierra was unwilling to open the ballet book till she finished her homework. What if her mum nipped up to check it, now that nothing mattered more than marks and grades? Gone were their cosy mother-daughter chats – and all because she had got into the *highly regarded* Roantree School last year. But with Rosella in the room, doing even the algebraic exercises she usually whizzed through was brain damaging.

Her schoolbag packed, Sierra still hesitated. Because of what had happened before, she couldn't put it past her mum to stick her head round the door to rule out any medical emergencies. Dash, she'd have to hold on till her parents went to sleep. She lay in bed with up to her chin under covers for a while, and then wriggled restlessly. Was there really a dancer inside the book under her bed? Or had her stressing about ballet made her imagination work overtime?

After what seemed like a week of nights, she heard the floorboards creak (Mum), next groan (Dad). Then she heard their door close.

The signal.

Sierra switched on her ballerina lamp. Down on fours, she reached into the darkness beneath her bed for the book. Holding her breath she turned to the page. *Yup!* With a finger on her lips now, she watched Rosella slip out. 'We've got to be quiet. But what did you want to say?'

'You see,' Rosella said, 'I was doing dance teacher training. I could train you for the audition.'

Sierra sniffed stardom. Here she was endeavouring to draw up a program for herself, and then this. 'Truly?' she asked, wondering whether she was having a dream.

But, again, Rosella was wearing that sparkly smile. 'Truly,' she said.

Seconds later, Sierra's heart sank. 'You can't train me here. Mum can't find out! She wants me to stop ballet and dive into my schoolwork. She's been on about my getting a *proper* job one day, a job with a future and everything. I know what that means. I saw it all in her eyes – me, with a stethoscope round my neck, a judge's wig on my head ... careers like that!' She did a thumbs-down. 'When I told her I wanted to move on to full-time ballet to become a dancer, she went psycho. You should have seen the *no* in her eyes, it was such a big no!'

Sierra's ears buzzed with her own furious words flying from her mouth in her frenzy.

'Not something else! Not something else! I *have* to be a dancer, I can't live without ballet!' she had yelled.

Rosella took Sierra's hands in hers.

'But if I get the lead role,' Sierra pressed on, 'Mum will feel bad about pulling me out of ballet. And it might show her that that's what I *should* do, really, really.' Her voice trembled. 'If I d-don't continue with my ballet classes, I won't be able to audition to g-get into a full-time program!'

'No good fretting about what might happen, Sierra. I had a dream too, but see how it panned out!' Rosella searched Sierra's face. 'Your best chance is to focus on *now*. And here you are, now, with me to train you. So let's work on getting you that part.'

Sierra wiped off her scowl with a smile, but was soon biting her lip. 'It's not just my mum. That was my brother who barged into the room. He'd come in even if I hung a do-not-disturb board on my door. We need a place with *no* people.'

'Yes, we don't want you getting into trouble.'

With no people ... no people ... no people ...

All at once, Sierra had it. The ideal spot. 'The Ghost House!' she said. 'That's the old empty house my cousin Toby and I explored a year ago. I'm sure, I'm sure, we didn't see any floaty characters or hear a wail.'

'I guess even ghosts can be tamed with a stellar performance,' Rosella said, her eyes flickering with mischief. 'Besides, ghosts won't knock me off dancing.'

'And the best part? No one will come there because of the rumours.'

'Is it nearby?'

'Fern Grove is a street off Pebbleridge Road, which is the way I walk home after school,' Sierra said. 'A funny sort of street with houses along only the first half. It narrowed into a lane, I think, and then twisted and turned until we got to the edge of the woods where the house was.'

Rosella held her head to one side looking thoughtful. 'How did you enter it?'

'Through an unlocked window at the back,' Sierra said, quickly crossing her fingers and hoping it remained unbolted as it had been then.

Outside, she heard heavy footsteps again. *Dad.* Seriously, should she have waited for a sleep noise like a snore before opening the book? Sierra closed it and crept into bed.

The Ghost House, here I come!

Chapter 4

On Monday, Sierra woke early and stuffed her ballet gear and *The Ballerina's Treasure Trove* at the bottom of her schoolbag, well hidden from her mum.

During the long day at school, her mind kept diverting to the Ghost House. Suppose that back window was locked now? Was there another way in? And what if Rosella wasn't there any more when she opened the book? What if this ... *strangeness* ... ceased as suddenly as it had begun?

∞

After school, she scurried up Pebbleridge Road to Fern Grove and got to the Ghost House. She waded through the rampant weeds, shivering at the thought of the murky alley that had led Toby and her to the window. How she wished there was a your-secret-is-safe-with-me type of soul who'd open the front door and let her in, although she had wanted a place with no people.

When she got to the end of the sprawling house, she squinted at the alley. Oh, no. It seemed longer than before. She shuffled her feet uncertainly. *Get moving*, her mind instructed. *How else are you going to follow your three-step plan?* She took a few deep breaths and turned in.

The trees shadowing the house became thicker and taller along the narrow path, taking her deeper into the gloom. Her footsteps slowing, she raised her eyes, searching for the sky which was hardly visible through the canopy of leaves.

The dry twigs and leaves under her feet crunched.

It was spooky. The sounds of the insects and birds were also off-key. Eerie.

Something slithered between her feet.

Sierra clenched her fists and stood rigid. *A snake?* Daringly, she looked down, and the relief made her light-headed. A lizard. It raised its neck, and Sierra saw its throat change colour. She chewed her lip. Was it telling her she shouldn't be here?

Come on Sierra, you can do it. You don't need Toby, she urged herself again, as she gave into an involuntary jitter. Then into her head plopped an idea. With no one around, she could open the book for Rosella right away and avoid being alone. Swiftly, she scrabbled in her bag for the book and flicked it to page 33, muttering, 'Be there, be there.'

Rosella stepped out with a crunch too, but it didn't crush her smile.

To Sierra, it felt like a burst of sunshine lifting the gloom.

'Oh, good, we're here,' Rosella said.

Her everything-is-as-normal, nothing-to-be-afraid-of attitude calmed Sierra. 'I hope we can get in through that window,' she said.

From the path, they entered another garden of brooding weeds surrounded by woods that were thicker than earlier.

'Ooh, Sierra, I'll run short of numbers if I count those windows. Which one was it?'

Sierra's eyes darted from one to the other to the last in the row. 'Toby named that part of the house *the ballroom!*' she said. With Rosella close behind her, she raced alongside the windows till she got to the enormous room Toby believed had been used for balls. She tugged at the first window. No. Together, they tried the others until they were at one with a missing plate of glass that was boarded up.

'*That's it!* How could I have forgotten? The unlocked window was right next.' Sierra yanked it, crying, 'Gateway, gateway, open for me.'

Rosella chuckled. 'You sound like Ali Baba calling, "Open Sesame".'

The window creaked.

Rosella joined her giving the window a jerk, and it moved.

'Neat!' Sierra said, when they got it wide open. Then she clung to the dusty windowsill, slung her leg over and climbed in with Rosella following suit. Surprise, surprise, unlike her classroom that appeared a teensy bit different on Monday mornings, nothing had altered in here in a year. The corner with the few bits of furniture was also the same. The sagging table, the rickety rocking chair, the chipped trunk ...

'A junk yard in a *ballroom!*' Rosella said, and then eagerly eyed the rest of the room. 'Empty, plenty of space. Wooden floors and walls lined with mirrors to correct yourself. Terrific!' She took Sierra by the waist and they waltzed round the place.

Sierra imagined violins *narrating* the 'Tales of the Vienna Woods'. Arrested by the highset ceiling, she pictured a chandelier with crystals of every conceivable shape.

Even after they stopped, breathless, Rosella twirled round the ballroom as if to ensure she hadn't missed any details. 'Look! There's a wooden rail at the other end. We can use it as a *barre*.'

'Like a real studio,' Sierra piped up.

On tiptoe, Rosella ran to the rail. She placed her left hand on it and did *pliés* in all five positions.

Miss Lana would have given her a *perfect*, Sierra reckoned, noting how Rosella did her knee bends with her legs turned out right from her hips. With Rosella's training, maybe she too could perfect her turnout, and, yay, become the envy of her ballet class.

Glad at not having to pass Miss Lana's *uniform code* test, Sierra wriggled into her tights and cerise leotard, put on her headband and removed her watch. She had to, had to, had to get home before her mum did. Quickly she sat on the floor and slipped on her pink leather ballet shoes, tying the drawstrings as fast as she could. Then she gave Rosella the thumbs-up seeing her complete an exercise.

'We have all we need,' Rosella said. 'We can manage without music.'

'Coming up,' Sierra said, reaching into her schoolbag with a grin. She held out an iPod.

'Sierra Ballerina, you've thought of everything!'

'*Music for Classical Ballet Class*,' Sierra said, and switched it on ...

As the music filled her body and spirit, Sierra slid into dance mode. She did her *pliés* with Rosella's in mind. Then she moved on with the rest of the *barre* exercises she'd learned at class, focussing on Rosella's advice and corrections.

'Unfold, keeping your supporting leg also well turned out ... that's right,' Rosella called, while Sierra was executing her *développés*.

After the *barrework*, they took to the middle of the ballroom for centre practice. Sierra couldn't believe it; this training program *was* the real deal. And it wasn't a dream.

Rosella first got her to do a *port de bras* exercise. 'Go on following your arms with your eyes ... and head ... that's ... the way ... Good,' she said.

Again, with more juicy pointers that quenched Sierra's thirst for perfection, Rosella helped her with her centre movements. 'Now try this,' she said, linking some of those steps and demonstrating a sequence.

Sierra marked it with her feet. *Glissade, glissade, assemblé* ...

Rosella said, 'Prepare.'

Then across the room Sierra glided, her heart as light as she was on her feet.

The training for her life-saving audition had started.

Chapter 5

On Saturday, Sierra left the dance centre with her heart soaring because her sessions with Rosella had got Miss Lana noticing *her*. *Voila!* Even Min, who was not totally into ballet, had observed the praises. Suppose she increased her practice time at home? After all, it was do or die.

She breezed along to Miss Lana's theme: 'The way to perfection is practise, practise, practise.' Okay, so she'd shift her white furniture to one side of her bedroom and, ouch, part with her beanbag seat till the audition was over, to create space. Now that home practice had taken on a whole new meaning, that's what she needed. Space.

∞

When Sierra got home, she rocketed upstairs to reorganise her room and her jaw dropped. 'Mum! What are you – what's this extra bed doing in my room?'

Her mum was tucking in a leafy patterned sheet. 'Grandma will be here any minute, sweetie. Dad has gone to fetch her.'

'Grandma? In my room? You didn't tell me she was coming.'

Her mum patted the mattress, looking pleased with her handiwork. 'Of course, I tried to the other day when you overreacted to my peeking at that ballet book.'

'But, but why *my* room?' Sierra cried. 'Doesn't she stay with Aunt Kelly when she comes to Sutherbrook?'

'Kelly is going to a conference and –'

'W-why couldn't she visit once Aunt Kelly got home?' Sierra blurted, regretting her words as soon as she said them.

Her mum fluffed up the pillows and then peered at Sierra as though she hadn't seen her before. 'You've been in another world of late. What's the matter with you, girl?'

Sierra rolled her tongue to lock in her speech; the girl-term meant her mum was about to get stuck into her.

'Do not grumble! It's only till Grandma's house is repaired. The leaks –'

Sierra was saved by her dad's entry. He walked in with a red suitcase in each hand and placed them on the wooden stand near her grandma's bed.

Sierra glared at her cramped bedroom. Dance? Fat chance.

'Another on the way,' he said, winking at Sierra with an eye that was as blue as hers.

Breathe? Fat chance.

He returned with a smaller bag made of a pinkie-beige floral fabric and set it on the floor next to her grandma's bed. 'Ready, for girl-talk?' he asked Sierra.

Sierra stretched her lips hoping they'd produce a smile. Her dad and his jokes – they spilt from his mouth without him knowing. Maybe that was why he didn't have any worry lines like those that creased her mum's forehead, she thought, watching them file out of her room.

Then before she could make head or tail of her transformed bedroom, in swept her grandma appearing more doll-like than usual, her slight frame lost in a dress made with tiers of pastel georgette. She threw her arms round Sierra with a flourish and smothered her with a trillion kisses, in spite of her ruffled collar getting in the way. 'Sierra, dear, those dimples of yours seem deeper each time I meet you.'

'But your dimples are the deepest I've seen, Grandma,' Sierra said, attempting to insert a welcome wave into her voice. Those dimples. That round face. That pointed nose. That straight back. Now the dress. All that was missing were some jerky movements to complete her grandma's doll disguise, Sierra figured, reflecting on Swanilda passing off as *Coppélia* ...

Ashamed at not wanting to share her room, she opened her cupboard and slid her clothes along the rail to one end to allow for her grandma's. She tapped her chest of drawers.

'For the things in that,' she said, and crossed to the flowery suitcase.

Her grandma's hands came down on the bag with a slam. 'Not this!' Her tone was higher than on other days and her eyelids fluttered at a frightening rate. 'Won't need it,' she said, shoving the suitcase under her bed. Then she flopped on the sheets with her fists in her lap and shut her eyes.

Sierra stood staring, a thousand theories circling in her head. What could it be? Had *she* upset her?

Moments later, her grandma was beaming. 'Now to unpack.'

Oops. How could a face go from happy to wretched to happy so fast? And since when did her grandma have mood swings? Sierra gave her clothes a final jab.

'See, Grandma, you can have half the rail and space at the bottom for your shoes,' she said, striving again to allay her qualms. Her grandma was fun; it was the timing of her visit that was lousy. 'Give me your keys. I'll get your clothes.'

'The bags aren't locked, dear. But don't you worry.'

Sierra sat at the edge of her grandma's bed, her eyes on the colourful mountain that was forming on it. Skirts, blouses, dresses and trousers in every shade. Next it was shoes: wedges, heels and flats with lots of straps. How *long* was she going to stay?

Then hand on chin, her grandma lingered over the unopened red suitcase on the stand. 'Tell you what, I'll leave that for later. It's just more of the same.'

More? *Ditch the reorganising, ditch the practising*, a little voice inside Sierra's head whispered.

After hanging her clothes, her grandma glanced round the room as if she had landed on foreign soil. 'Coral pink. Such a gorgeous colour. Haven't been in here for a while.' She eyed the pictures on the wall.

'Got them last month,' Sierra said, following her gaze. 'Anna Pavlova and Margot Fonteyn – my dream is to be like them.'

'A silly dream, dear, when only a few get to the top. Give it up, I say.'

'*Give up?*' Sierra's knees went weak. Nobody got her. Even her grandma was being a ballet grouch like her mum. 'Never!' she said. 'I will become one of those few.'

Her grandma wasn't listening to her protests. Bending, she was thrusting her floral suitcase further under the bed. She straightened with that wretched look on her face.

'Er, what's in that bag?' Sierra asked, wondering why it was getting her all fidgety and stressed out.

'Old bits and pieces.' Again her grandma sounded shrill.

Sierra pricked up her ears. Something *was* the matter. Why else would she act weird? 'If you won't be using that stuff, why did you bring –'

'My house is in a mess.'

'But if the things are old ...'

Her grandma waved away the comment and was smiling once more, ambling across to Sierra's bookcase with a stack of Agatha Christie mysteries. 'To feed my reading habit,' she said.

'The shelves are full.' Sierra failed to trim the curt edge in her voice because she was still hurt by her grandma's stance on her ballerina dreams. Wouldn't *anybody* support her?

Hither and thither her grandma moved Sierra's books, rearranging them until she was able to slot in her novels.

Sierra raised her eyes to the ceiling. *The Ballerina's Treasure Trove* wasn't safe here; she'd have to sneak it out of her private-collections drawer and hide it at the Ghost House. She gave an inward sigh at the setback in her do-or-die effort and then perked up. All right, she couldn't practise at home, but she had her real-deal training with Rosella.

What she didn't have was even a clue to the mystery under her grandma's bed.

Chapter 6

After school on Monday, Sierra made her way to the Ghost House, reassessing the situation. Fair enough, she wouldn't have to shelve home practice if she used the family room. The thing was that it had already become her grandma's reading den, so it would be like queuing for her turn. How ridiculous was that? Add to it, Rory peeping from here, there and everywhere with that caught-you-doing-the-soppy-soppy grin whenever she danced a sequence around the house. *Gross!*

When she got to the Ghost House, her heart lifted. Away from prying eyes, she could at least be *Sierra*. The real one. She hoisted herself through the window of the ballroom, got on her attire and opened the ballet book to greet a smiling Rosella. Then not wanting to waste even a second of her time here, she started warming up at the *barre*.

'Your *pirouettes* are coming on well,' Rosella remarked, giving the session a run down at the end. 'Spinning on one leg does require perfect balancing. And isn't keeping your eyes firmly fixed on a spot the trick to avoid dizziness! Now, let's see. We've got till the end of this term, haven't we?'

'Yup, the audition is on the Saturday before the last class for the term.' Sierra slipped off her headband and knocked her hair into place with her fingers. 'True, I'm not trying out for a role in a professional ballet production or anything. But I'm lucky Miss Lana decided to have an audition for solos rather than picking students on past-performance. I heard her telling a mum that doing it this way will make *everyone* practise hard. She wants to put on the best ever show. Of course you know why landing Princess Aurora is big-time for me – can't think of another idea to get Mum off my case.' Sierra swallowed hard. 'I could end up like the Dying Swan.'

Rosella's face softened in sympathy. 'Oh, Sierra, told you it's fruitless to worry about the future, which is never certain. As I said, pay attention to the moment. That means not dwelling on the past also.'

'Is that why you don't agonise over what happened to you?' Sierra asked.

'Absolutely. What's gone is gone.'

Sierra drew a long breath as though she was scrabbling for some of Rosella's wisdom. 'Thanks heaps for today. But I really must work on how to pull you out of this book. For real, for good. The two-hour deadline sucks!'

'Don't even try!' A glint of panic showed in Rosella's eyes.

'I go on thinking, thinking of that mistake the witch made in her *no-way-out* spell,' Sierra cried. 'Could there be a loophole in that error which might free you?'

'Again, as I said, Azra will come after me and make me disappear. With her living forever, that threat will *always* hang over me.'

Sierra felt her eyes welling with tears.

'I see you're still distressed about me.' Concern poured from Rosella's blue-green eyes. 'This issue is getting to you. Do you want to skip our sessions for a week or two?'

'Not at all,' Sierra said. 'But how can I live as if everything is fine when you're stuck in a book? It eats me inside to see you on the page and to think that we can do *nothing*!'

'Listen, Sierra.' Rosella cupped Sierra's face in her palm and wiped the tears that had escaped. 'It's not your fault I'm trapped in a book. It's not your fault my breaking away from it is risky. So stop feeling bad. In fact, you're fulfilling *my* dream.'

'*I am?*'

'You are. You returned ballet to my life. It's not only that I get to do my favourite moves and sequences ... I get to train a talented dancer like you which is rewarding for me because I wanted to be a ballet teacher. That's the reason I was doing teacher training.' Rosella blinked, looking aside. 'Been a long while since I trained a dancer ...'

Sierra saw a sole tear trickle down Rosella's pale cheek. That was a first.

'I owe you, Sierra Ballerina,' she whispered.

'I owe *you*,' Sierra echoed.

'You see? Friendship is about helping each other,' Rosella said. 'And we must follow our dreams from wherever!'

∞

At dinner that night, to take her mind off her anxiety and the book, which on account of her grandma she'd left behind inside the trunk in the ballroom, Sierra indulged in Saturday's ballet class.

Getting a *perfect* for her *pas de bourrées* was striking gold, she reckoned, because they had to do those little linking steps in a lot of their sequences. Sure enough, Cindy and Stacy too were collecting the compliments, yet it was nice to belong to that tribe. Then Evan's smiles. Not that she liked him or something, she told herself, ignoring the fierceness of her denial. But being a good dancer he could well be cast Prince Florimund, and if she was – ooh, wondrously – allotted Princess Aurora, they'd be dance partners. Ah, *pas de deux*. Had Evan also pictured them in a dance for two? Is that why he had smiled?

'Now that Dad's job is coming to an end, we have to be careful,' her mum said, reining in on her thoughts.

'*Dad?*' Sierra sat up in her chair.

Her dad guzzled the last drop of water in his glass. 'Well, we were told today that the Athena West Insurance takeover *is* going through, which means our section will be non-existent in three months.'

'Will we go hungry?' Rory squealed.

Their mum ruffled his hair. 'We'll see that you have grub! The difficulty will be to put you into a better school. Oh, Sierra, your scholarship is a saviour.'

Her mum was gazing at her with those *proper* jobs in her eyes.

Sierra's stomach churned. 'But, but can't you get another job, Dad?'

'I'll have to – won't I? – to fill four snarling tummies,' he joked, but he didn't wink or anything.

Sierra peered at him. Was that a worry line on his forehead? Why did this have to happen? Why couldn't it be normal? Poor Dad.

Her mum sighed in a breathy, noisy sort of manner. 'Unlikely that I'll get more hours of work at the salon. Fortunately, your education at Roantree is taken care of, sweetie –'

'Don't go wasting too much of your time on other activities, dear,' her grandma intervened.

The apple crumble on Sierra's tongue suddenly tasted bitter. Statements like that were only going to make her mum think she was right about her decision on ballet. Sierra was already sensing the eyes around the table regarding her with a *no*, a no for ballet.

To dodge those eyes, she kept hers fixed on her bowl. But that voice in her head was chasing her, hounding her, saying, *with your dad unemployed your family will struggle, and Rory with a poor education might have to queue for his supper, so you need to be practical, consider your career options, surely you know better* ... As if to attack her dilemma, she dug her spoon into the apple crumble. She couldn't raise it to her mouth, though, because there was also a spark igniting inside her. Anger, anger ...

If her grandma could butt into her life, why couldn't she butt into her grandma's?

While the others were still talking, the rest of her dessert untouched, she sped upstairs and into her room. She pushed away the niggle of guilt that had arisen in her mind from knowing it was wrong to snoop. Then she squatted by her grandma's bed and dragged out her well-guarded suitcase.

She glared at the wee padlock that got in her way. *You said the bags weren't locked, Grandma! So why lock the bag with the old things?*

Chapter 7

Dressed in a black leotard and ballet skirt, Miss Lana waited till Mr Trotter got to the piano.

'The old wheels giving a bit of bother,' he said, adjusting the piano stool.

Sierra glanced at the studio clock. Lucky Mr Trotter. He'd been spared the punctuality-is-rule-number-one-at-the-Lana-Lott-Dance-Centre look: Miss Lana was *not* peering down her hooked nose.

She was focussing on the students at the *barre*. 'Class, Kim Hasler is starting with us today. She comes with excellent reports from her previous ballet school.'

Sierra eyed the newcomer who had taken the slot right in front of her because Min hadn't shown up. Her hand was raised in a royal-like wave, and her feet in first position were turned out to form a straight line.

'I've already told her about the syllabus and agenda for this year – the audition, the concert,' Miss Lana continued. She nodded at Mr Trotter for music. '*Pliés*. And ...' she said to the class, and then began pacing the studio calling out to them. 'Knees ... legs ... your turnout ... bend ... rise ... stomach in ...'

Sierra was eager to get to the *barre* exercises she'd listed in her ballet journal as she'd been practising them with Rosella. But when she got to them, trouble brewed because she ruined the speed of her *frappés* by peeking at Kim's foot to check whether she was striking faster, and then with her *grands battements*, lost the sweep in her kick seeing Kim going higher. *Drop Kim from your mind!* she scolded herself.

Next they had to work through the sequence Miss Lana was demonstrating at the *barre*. Sierra saw Kim watching their teacher intently. Then without even

40

marking it, the girl flowed from step to step as if she'd rehearsed it a dozen times. Sierra's heart puckered. Grasping a combination in a tick like that was a *big* plus at an audition.

'Now to the centre,' Miss Lana said.

Everybody tiptoed to the middle of the studio and got into rows. Sierra slid into the first. *Adage* was her favourite; she loved slow movements. Oh, grand, Miss Lana was pointing Kim to a place behind. Sierra loosened up. And when she got to the *arabesque*, she happily confirmed that out of sight did really mean *out of mind*. No distractions, no wobbles.

'Lovely,' Miss Lana said to Sierra. In a moment she said, 'Perfect,' to Kim.

Sierra's supporting leg shook.

Imagine you're at the audition, she commanded herself strictly, fighting to keep dancing like the rest as the music rippled through the studio. But when Miss Lana got on to counting the beats and doing the steps in a sequence for centre practice, she snapped back to dance mode and marked it with her feet as well as her arms. She would *not* let Kim outshine her another time.

Then a wave at Mr Trotter and Miss Lana said, 'And ...'

With that, the first row took off across the studio.

'Lovely the way you move to the music, your heart is in it,' Miss Lana said, when Sierra got to the other end.

Sierra soaked up the praise with a grin; she'd captured Miss Lana's hawk eyes. No sooner, though, she noticed the glimmer in those critical eyes as they followed Kim performing the sequence. Mr Trotter was no better. He was twisting his neck to catch a glimpse of Kim while he tapped a tune, and he had a faint smile on his plump, red face.

Sierra tried to banish those Kim-the-idol images from her mind. When she got to the *pirouettes*, however, she couldn't as much as keep her eyes on one spot. *Arrrggghhh!* Hadn't it been easy-peasy doing them for Rosella?

Now Sierra was swaying.

'Spot! Spot!' Miss Lana was on to her.

But Sierra's swinging had put her completely off-balance; she had to stop.

Miss Lana hailed Kim. 'Show us the *pirouette*, please,' she said.

Sierra squirmed. A new girl demonstrating for her? She made herself stare, grappling to keep her face expressionless, although she wanted to drag her headband over her eyes when Kim pushed on to the ball of her left foot to turn.

Then Sierra was told to practise the correction, and all eyes settled on her. She hissed at the ground to split and suck her in.

After that fiasco, she joined a group for *allegro*, anxious to impress with her jumps. She soooo needed to win back Miss Lana's approval because the audition wasn't that far off.

Yet this part of the class too finished with Showtime for Kim.

Kim leapt diagonally across the studio, leaving Sierra taunted by those *grands jetés*. Like splits in the air, she cried under her breath. But she didn't want to mask her eyes as before – it was the love-ballet thing. Here was a serious dancer, a dancer who believed in perfecting each step.

And ... a dancer who was easing into the role of Princess Aurora.

Ouch, how could Rosella tell her not to brood about what might *be*? *But weren't those the very thoughts that messed with your ballet?* that voice inside Sierra challenged her, adding to her exasperation. Glad it was time for the *révérence*, she curtseyed to thank Miss Lana.

It didn't somehow look as if the class had ended.

Miss Lana was clapping for their attention. Why wasn't she allowing in her next class? Didn't everything around here usually happen like clockwork? Sierra held back while the others clustered around Miss Lana, and Cindy and Stacy threaded their way to the front with Kim in tow.

'Final call for the day,' Miss Lana said. 'We want one of you to enter the Junior Showcase National Ballet Competition. Apart from the experience, winning a prestigious competition like this might be useful if you're hoping to apply to get into a full-time ballet school.'

This was neat. Sierra moved up a little and amid the 'oohs and ahs' lifted her hand. 'Miss Lana, how will you select someone?'

Miss Lana's eyes journeyed from face to face as if to alert them to listen carefully. 'Well,' she said, 'the audition will assist us to make that decision.'

A swell of aspiration put a spring in Sierra's step as she wove her way to the front too. The audition was not only about the concert any longer; it was also about a national comp. Even her mum had to realise this was *mega* – here was her chance.

Then her heart plummeted.

Now there was *Kim*.

At the noticeboard, everyone crowded around Kim. Seriously. Did they have to let her feel she was the Goddess of Dance? Soon, unable to resist, Sierra joined the fold.

It was then that she saw another Kim-the-idol image. Evan.

He awarded Kim a smile that was as refreshing as the crisp white tee-shirt he wore with his black tights. 'Enjoy?' he asked her.

Kim's ebony eyes twinkled as if he was *her* Prince Florimund. 'Cool, right?' she said, giving her bun a tug and a pat though every detail about her was perfect. Then she giggled.

Sierra scoffed. Did she think Evan was going to be taken in by that titter? He'd back away any minute. Perhaps he'd wink at *her* to indicate that he was on her side.

Evan didn't budge; he didn't even blink.

'We shifted from Glacyvale only a few days ago,' Kim chatted on. 'But I didn't want to waste any time.'

Of course she wouldn't. This girl was keen; this girl was ready. She also had Miss Lana mesmerised. Sierra slipped off, dispirited.

With Kim hogging the limelight, how was she going to succeed at the audition to talk her mum into letting her do ballet?

Chapter 8

How very odd, Sierra thought, at school on Monday morning when she didn't hear the click of the stilettos along the passage until three minutes past the starting bell. Not like Ms Hart.

'Good morning, girls. Sorry I'm late,' she said, now entering the class. She wasn't alone.

Following her to the front of the room, chin up and all, was a new student.

She was Kim Hasler.

Sierra dug her palms into her desk. More of *her*?

'Kim Hasler is joining our class,' Ms Hart said. 'She's moved to Sutherbrook with her family, and we must see that she settles in.' She beamed at everyone as though their class had got lucky.

Sierra rolled her eyes. Was Kim going to be the idol of Year Six as well?

Kim dished out her royal wave. Again, there was no slouching or anything – she was posture perfect. She appeared capable of remaining like that even in her sleep.

'I'll give you a moment to get acquainted with Kim while I hop across to speak to Mr Wheeler next door,' Ms Hart said. 'But keep your voices down.'

Sierra busied herself with her books, not Kim.

Kim, however, wedged her way through the rows of desks and got to her. 'Hi there. Fancy seeing you here. Ballet buddies and class buddies, right?'

'Yup, seems like it. So you're new here?'

'Yah. Dad started work at the Sutherbrook Hospital. He's a doctor.'

'Hope you'll like it here,' Sierra said, wishing she wouldn't.

'It's cool, this place. Real cool.'

Cool? Year Six? Roantree? Or Sutherbrook? What would be cool, Sierra determined, was if Kim erupted in bumps (big ones) that put her in quarantine till after the audition.

Instead, Kim kept on looking like the alabaster figurine of a ballerina. 'But the coolest is Miss Lana's announcement on Saturday,' she said. 'A national competition! And doing Princess Aurora – wouldn't that be a dream?'

'The thing is we've got semester exams cropping up just before the audition,' Sierra said. *If Kim would at least catch the study bug!*

'Exams?' Kim pouted. 'Not into fractions, decimals or whatever! Won't need that stuff, not as a ballet dancer.'

Sierra forced a smile. Kim had it easy. Schoolwork wasn't *her* choice either, but she had to keep up with it to hold on to her scholarship. Glad to see Min sailing over to them, Sierra lurched at her as if she had spotted an escape route.

But Kim latched on to them.

'Hiya,' Min said. 'Sounds as if you're the latest addition to our ballet class Sierra was splitting to tell me about this morning. Our Sierra Seldon, here, is also going to be a dancer.'

'Yah? And you too?'

'Nope. No ballerina dreams for me!' Min swept her fringe away from her eyes. 'Going to audition for our concert, though. My sister is the star in the senior show, so that means I've got to get even a short solo for ours!'

'Didn't see you on Saturday,' Kim said.

'Had the cough-cold thingy.'

Kim helped herself to the book on Sierra's desk. '*Margot Fonteyn*. You are into ballet! What else have you got?'

'A few –'

'Tell her about that second-hand book,' Min interrupted. 'It seemed good. *The Ballerina's Treasure* something, wasn't it?'

'Got a few books with exercises,' Sierra said, raising her voice to drown Min's. She gave Min a shut-your-mouth look.

'Exercises for practising? My dad's promised to fix a mini *barre* in the spare room. Then I'll have a home studio,' Kim said.

Sierra bottled a grin. Yippee, she had the Ghost House plus Rosella.

'And with the concert, Mum wants to whisk me off to order satin ballet shoes,' Kim added.

'Oh.' Sierra pictured Kim's parents rising from the audience and clapping till their hands throbbed as their daughter received curtain call after call. How good it had to be. The very backing *she* yearned for. Her inside felt hollow and then it filled with loneliness.

'Bet you're also gunning for the main ones!' Kim said, jerking Sierra out of her daydream.

'Sierra's a Princess Aurora hopeful,' Min volunteered.

Sierra shrugged and wrinkled her nose as if to say, *I'm not too fussed*. How could Min *not* get the message? Seriously.

Kim's eyes dimmed, but she giggled, this time tossing her head back in a way that sent her long dark plaits flying. 'You're good, Sierra, real good.' She emerged from another bout of giggles and turned to Min. 'Had to demonstrate the *pirouettes* for Sierra.'

Get over it! Sierra steamed at the mouth.

'*Pirouettes?*' Min frowned. 'But she's usually –'

'Miss Lana kept giving me *perfects*,' Kim batted on.

Full of herself. Sierra nearly said it aloud.

Kim treated Sierra to a sugary smile. 'Why don't you come home on Sunday to watch *The Sleeping Beauty*? Got the Paris Opera Ballet and the Bolshoi version. Your pick.'

'Have both,' Sierra said. She wasn't going to be fooled by the buddy talk. She'd heard the strand of defiance woven into Kim's overdone giggle when Min told her that Sierra was after the same thing. And this fake smile ... What more?

'Then why don't you bring along *The Ballerina's Treasure* book?' Kim's voice had also become sickeningly sweet. 'We could do the exercises in it together. There must be lots, right?'

She wants to see what I'm practising! Sierra's lip curled in disgust.

Ms Hart rushed in. 'Girls! Let's get started, took longer than I expected. Sierra, I can see you've taken Kim under your wing. She can have the empty seat next to you.'

Sierra stood rooted to the ground. It was as though Kim was following her around, inching closer and closer, to remind her of what she was up against.

Chapter 9

'Did the new girl have anything to do with why you were kicking higher and higher with your *grands battements*?' Rosella asked Sierra, after their session at the Ghost House. 'It's not only a case of going higher – you know you have to keep your supporting leg absolutely straight.'

Sierra knew it was seeing Kim go sky-high at class that had egged her on. Whoops, had her face turned flame red? How could she have let that girl get to her without even *being* here? 'Kim is a bigger problem than Cindy or Stacy,' she said, 'because she is perfect!'

'And you dance with passion.' Rosella smiled reassuringly. 'You were meant to be a ballerina!'

Sierra went all gooey inside. Rosella was the only person who understood her. Really. 'Mum's eyebrows will shoot up her forehead if I'm chosen for the comp. My grand scheme to be allowed to stay on at ballet might actually work!'

'More reason not to spoil your technique,' Rosella said. 'You'll be marked down.'

Sierra crossed Kim out of her mind several times and then gave Rosella a hug. 'Today's extra-long practice was spot-on for stepping up, which is what I have to do with Kim and the comp now on my plate. You're the best! Wish I could –'

'Training you allows me to hold on to my dream, told you, didn't I?' Rosella seemed to know exactly what Sierra was thinking. 'I'm safer in the book.'

'Yup,' Sierra said, but she didn't feel that yup in her heart.

∞

'Sweetie, you've been working hard,' her mum said that evening. 'Grandma was concerned that you were coming home late. Those afterschool tutorials, isn't it?'

'Er ... got semester exams to tackle.'

'Guessed it was that!' Her mum plucked the mustard yellow envelope that was propped up against the Rory-plus-Dad photo on the kitchen shelf and handed it to her.

Sierra opened it and the guilt that sprang from her heart stifled the grin that should have adorned her face. *The Nutcracker.* Two tickets to her best-of-the-best ballet. 'But *why*, Mum?'

'Getting your priorities right, I can see. Most kids don't want to spend their afterschool time at tutorials.'

The pride in her eyes nearly made Sierra throw up her arms and confess. 'But, but, how can you manage these tickets?' she stammered. 'With Dad's job –'

'Not to worry, sweetie,' her mum said, now eyeing her to-do list that was stuck on the fridge door among Rory's racing car magnets.

'But Mum –'

'You could take Min.'

'But –'

'I could ask Mrs Chan if you like, spoke to her only the other day. She said Min was finding those tutorials very helpful. The science –'

'I don't go for the science tutorials,' Sierra said, nervous that Mrs Chan might get to know, through Min, that she didn't attend them, and let on. She couldn't have her mum getting suspicious and digging into unearth her whereabouts.

The Nutcracker ... Nutcracker!

She soooo wanted to see it, but it was meant to be a reward for doing extra schoolwork. Not extra ballet training. *And with your dad unemployed soon, it should be additional schoolwork, not additional ballet, you'd think,* that little voice in her interjected, spoiling everything. Sierra swallowed the lump in her throat. 'A neat surprise, Mum. But not at this price. Can't you return these tickets?'

'No, and no buts. You'll love it, sweetie.'

'I know. Er ...' Even the thought of a journey through the Land of Snow to the Kingdom of Sweets with Clara and the Nutcracker Prince couldn't ease Sierra's conscience.

But tickets to the ballet!

As a reluctant smile of pleasure curved her lips, her grandma padded into the kitchen. 'Tickets ... ah, *The Nutcracker*. Ballet, how lovely.'

'As an interest,' Sierra's mum chimed in.

An interest? Are you serious? Sierra felt her happy lips droop.

'You've got into a great school, dear,' her grandma said, as though Sierra needed reminding.

Her mum nodded at Sierra. Oh, no. Those eyes were hinting again at *proper* jobs. Why did her grandma have to bring on the Roantree pitch? At this rate, she'd never get a *yes* for ballet. And with the exams looming, if her mum decided to stop Sierra's ballet classes right now, instead of next term, she wouldn't be able to audition for the concert.

Then her moment to win over her mum would be stuffed!

Sierra scooted from the kitchen, not daring to wait, not daring to find out. On her way to the staircase, by the laundry door, she saw something shiny on the floor. Craving for anything that would brighten her dark hour, she knelt beside it.

A key.

She picked it and blinked to clear her hazy eyes, and then read the letters on the frayed tag attached to the bronzy key ring: 'JT'. Could it be a name? Like, like

Jennifer? Oh, well, the letters still didn't add up. Her grandma was Jennifer *Parkes*. Her heart thumped. *Why, of course!*

Her grandma's maiden name was *Tuckey*.

JT for Jennifer Tuckey.

Sierra landed on her feet, recalling her grandma arriving with her red suitcases unlocked. Was this then the key to her mystery bag?

Chapter 10

Two steps in a go. Sierra lunged up the stairs and crossed the room in giant strides. Crouching, she hauled the bag from under her grandma's bed and thrust the key into the padlock.

It sprang open.

Yes! Guiltily, she glanced over her shoulder and listened to ensure that no one was coming, and then unzipped the bag. A black cloth tucked in neatly on all four sides concealed whatever was beneath. She peeled it off cautiously.

Parcels – wrapped in once-white tissue now creamed with time.

What were they?

Frowning, she lifted the package on top. It weighed almost nothing: a kind of fabric, maybe? She removed the sheets of fragile paper, one by one, taking care not to tear them and noting exactly how they were folded so she could put them back as they were.

Then gasping, she stared at the contents until her eyes almost popped out.

A tutu!

About her own size. What was her *grandma* doing with it? Quickly, but mindfully, she undid another pack.

Faded leotards.

What? Did she do *ballet*? Flabbergasted, but still doing her level best not to be clumsy, Sierra opened yet another.

Tattered ballet shoes.

She gaped at the things she had fished out. Her grandma, a dancer? Nonsense. Far-fetched. But if these weren't hers, why would she cling to them? And, and, why hadn't they been binned, instead of being packed like priceless possessions?

There had to be an explanation, it had to be in here, and she had to find it, and fast. She checked the door again, even sniffing for a wisp of the jasmine fragrance of her grandma's regular perfume. Feeling it would be bad to unwrap everything, she rummaged through the suitcase, her heart drumming to an unknown tune. Ouch. Something sharp. A corner. She grabbed it and tugged. Into her hand slipped a beige folder with decorative gold letters spelling 'Jennifer Tuckey' at the centre top.

Please, please, *explain*, she implored silently, flicking the folder open.

Newspaper clippings.

She read the title of the first: *'Ballet success for thirteen-year-old Jennifer Tuckey'*.

Sierra blinked in astonishment and then devoured the piece.

Jennifer Tuckey won first place at the Starline National Ballet Competition last evening, held annually in aid of the Starline Children's Hospital. A promising young ballerina, Jennifer danced with a style and technique well beyond her years ...

Her grandma a national champion? No-no. There had to be a mix-up; this had to be some other Jennifer Tuckey. But why would she keep the clipping if it wasn't about her? Sierra's mind ran helter-skelter as she skimmed the next lot to get to the bottom of her discovery. Each one was on Jennifer Tuckey's ballet triumphs.

Tuckey stole the show in her role as Snow White at the Fraser Dance School's annual concert ...

As the star in Alice in Wonderland, Jennifer captivated the audience ...

Jennifer Tuckey's performance as Coppélia was legendary ...

Coppélia? Sierra had finally found what appeared vaguely possible with her grandma's doll-like characteristics and everything. She reread the yellowed cutting. Still unconvinced, she plugged away at the pictures in the articles, although unaware of what her grandma had looked like as a girl. The fact that the photos had dulled with time didn't help, but certain features were obvious in all of them. Round face, pointed nose, longish dimples ...

Her grandma.

Sierra closed her eyes, gutted by a mixture of disbelief and betrayal. 'Why, why, *why*, didn't you tell me I was following in your footsteps, Grandma?'

'I couldn't,' came the reply.

Sierra put down the folder and leapt to her feet. 'Grandma! I found the key and –'

Her grandma's shoulders sagged and her body began to shake. That straight-backed doll had transformed into a feeble old lady right before Sierra's eyes.

'Let me!' Sierra darted to her and placed an arm around her waist. 'I'm sorry, I'm sorry, I opened your bag. I know I shouldn't have.' She led her grandma to the bed. 'Here you are, sit.'

A tear ran down her grandma's cheek. Sierra wiped it with her thumb and sat by her. 'Now I know how ballet got into me. Neat, Grandma. You were what I want to be. A national champion! A star!'

Her grandma lugged in a shuddery breath. 'Shoosh, dear. I was no star. I was a little fool who imagined I could be.' She lifted Sierra's chin with her finger and eyed her squarely. 'Life plays cruel pranks on us, dear. I've been trying to warn you. It took only a few seconds to shatter my dream.'

'But how? What happened?'

Her grandma buried her face in her hands and Sierra heard her muffled sobs, and then saw the anguish in her eyes when she raised her head.

'An ankle injury, when I was thirteen,' she said.

'Oh, Grandma! Did it happen at your ballet class?'

Her grandma stiffened, and her saddened face gave way to a peculiar expression.

Whoops, Sierra mouthed. Shouldn't she have asked? But why not?

'The specialist said, "No more ballet for you, young lady."' Her grandma's voice also sounded out of whack.

'Too bad!' Sierra said, putting off her unanswered question. This was *so* not the time to push it, even though there seemed more to the mystery.

'Sharing your room with its presence of ballet was like reliving my childhood,' her grandma plodded on. 'Got the jitters, dear, watching you harbour the very same ambition. But attempting to change your mind was perhaps wrong.'

'I guess it was to protect me,' Sierra said. 'And now that I know why, it is okay, Grandma. Honestly, it is.'

Her grandma stared miserably at her opened suitcase. 'All I have is a past I've packed into that bag. The fragments of my perished dream. I couldn't bear to leave it behind.'

Sierra's heart melted. Clearly, her grandma hadn't healed. Was it because she was hanging on to her past? Didn't Rosella say, what was gone was gone?

Now there was a faraway look in her eyes. 'The others wanted me to lighten up. They said there were plenty of things I could do, apart from ballet.'

Sierra boiled inside. She knew, slap-bang, how her grandma would have felt – didn't *she* resent anyone belittling her ballerina dreams? Suggesting she do something else?

Her grandma shook her head slowly. 'You have to have ballet shoes on to understand, you have to.'

'Of course! Only a dancer knows the virtue of turnout, the bliss of perfecting a step.' Sierra tucked her arm in her grandma's. 'Or the crippling anxiety of forgetting a sequence.' How could she have been vexed with her grandma? How could she? 'But you had a good life with Granddad, didn't you?' she asked, ferociously hoping that her grandma had found another reason to live.

'Oh, yes. And my two lovely girls, your mother and Kelly.' Her grandma lowered her voice as though she didn't want even the furniture to hear what she was about to tell Sierra. 'But when I lost ballet, I lost my heart too. I didn't want that to happen to you in *any* way. It's not just talent and technique, dear. In the next few years you may find you've grown too big, too tall. Not everyone can fit into the mould of a ballerina.'

Sierra tried to stamp out what her grandma was saying, but when she peeked at herself in the mirror, the reflection she saw made no promises. Why hadn't this possibility occurred to her? But what she *had* thought of, and stashed away in a not-to-be-visited corner of her mind, demanded to be heard. 'Suppose I *don't* get picked for full-time training by any ballet school?' she whispered.

Suddenly, her mum's tut-tutting about schoolwork and a good education didn't seem like a drag. It seemed like a caring mother's concern.

Chapter 11

When the last school bell clanged, Sierra smiled inwardly. Her mum and her grandma were going to be out and about for hours. So, yup, she could sneak into the house before them even if she got in one of those extra-long, need-to-beat-Kim training sessions with Rosella.

She hastened along Pebbleridge Road, picturing Kim practising twenty-four/seven for the audition while she had to squeeze in her exam revision as well. Okay, okay, her mum was right about schoolwork. Her eyes stung as if hot thorny bits had got into them. Her life was not about what *she* wanted. It was unfair. Why couldn't she be Kim with her do-as-I-please life?

Then something unsettled her. Was she being spied on? Nosy Kim? Clutching her breath, she glanced around her.

The intruder was her grandma.

Sierra quickened her step. Too late, she'd been spotted. Her grandma was peering at her from a window at Reads. Oh, no, she was waving heartily. Not wanting to arouse suspicion, Sierra waved back and dragged her feet to the glass door of the second-hand bookshop. Now she could see her mum in there also; how was she going to wriggle out of this one?

She entered the shop.

Mrs Vickers raised her eyes from the cash register at the tinkle of the doorbell and smiled at Sierra. Patting her mop of silver curls, she turned to Sierra's grandma who was picking her way to the counter. 'There's the *new* owner of your ballet book,' she said, pointing at Sierra.

Sierra watched the blood drain from her grandma's face, and her eyes widen with shock and then bulge with horror. The magazines in her hand slipped through her fingers and thudded to the floor. '*Sierra?*' She took a few hesitant steps and swayed.

Mrs Vickers rushed forward and held her up. 'Help!' she called, looking desperately towards Sierra's mum.

Sierra's heart bounced inside her. The book, her *grandma's*? *Her* grandma's? But, but then ... if, if –

Her mind crumbled ...

And she knew she wouldn't be able to piece herself together again without a clarification to this deepening mystery. She licked her dry lips and said nothing, though, realising that querying would only upset her grandma even more than she was. So seeing her in good hands, Sierra bolted out of the shop, unnoticed amid the chaos, and headed to the Ghost House for an answer to the question that was hanging from her tongue.

If *The Ballerina's Treasure Trove* had belonged to her grandma, did she *know* Rosella?

Chapter 12

At the Ghost House ballroom, Sierra dipped into the trunk for the ballet book and then flipped it to page 33. With bated breath she watched the forming shadow, her mouth poised.

'The previous owner of this book was supposed to be my grandma!' she burst out as soon as she saw Rosella.

'*Your grandma?*' Rosella sent her a narrow-eyed look of confusion. 'How do you – the dimples!' she exclaimed.

'You knew her!'

'Felt an uncanny connection to the past, that first day I saw you with *your* dimples.'

'But, but how –'

'Jenny got the book as a gift for her twelfth birthday. And I trained her.'

'*Trained* her?' Sierra cried. 'You said you stayed eighteen because you didn't age inside the book, but, but Grandma is sixty-two now. *You've been in the book for at least fifty years!*' She winced. 'Oh, Rosella. This situation is gruesome, worse than I thought. When you mentioned training a dancer, I assumed you were referring to what you did before you got trapped. Wasn't I a clot?'

'Hey, hey, Sierra Ballerina,' Rosella shushed, tilting her head. 'How could you have known the gory details when I didn't tell you? If I did, you'd have persisted with trying to get me out of the book. Pointless, as I said, with worst-of-the-worst spells that others can't break.'

'Th-then you must know,' Sierra said, 'how Grandma injured her ankle!'

'Her ankle?' Rosella whispered. Her face clouded, and she lowered her eyes to the ground. 'Er ... she fractured it while I was training her.'

'*No! No!*' Sierra clutched her cheeks with both hands. Why did it have to happen like that? Oh, why? Oh, why? No wonder her grandma chose to be mysterious about the question on whether she'd got hurt at her ballet class. How could she tell anyone a story like this? Who would have believed her?

Rosella's shoulders slumped as though she was changing her posture to renounce the dancer in her. 'It took only a minute, you see. There was no stopping it, there was no saving her ... But I never forgot her. What grace – the way she always held her head, her arms. And, oh, those feet, made for ballet.' Her eyes sought Sierra's, and she reached forward to touch her hand. 'A renowned ballerina, was she? Was she?'

'*You mean you don't know?*'

'Jenny didn't open the book after her injury, so I didn't see her. Tell me! Also how you found out –'

Voices.

Footsteps.

In the hallway outside the ballroom.

With a kick Sierra shut the ballet book and glanced round wildly for a hiding place.

Nowhere.

Her gaze fell on the trunk. She gathered up the book and her schoolbag, and sprinted to it. As she scrambled in with the bag, the book slipped from her hand, sliding across the floor.

She groaned mutely and pulled the lid of the trunk closed over her. *Don't come in here, don't come in here,* she begged.

But now the voices were inside the ballroom.

Oh, no. If they saw the book they'd scout about the premises. She'd have to listen out. Darn, this lid. It was muffling the talk.

'Suit ... for ... guesthouse ...' a thin-voiced man said.

Sierra tried not to breathe, hoping to gather more of the conversation. But her ears got clogged by a cough that followed.

Then another male with a gruff voice: 'High ceilings ... airy ... quiet area ... Craig Properties has ...'

Craig? The estate agent on Pebbleridge Road? Ah, the other person had to be a buyer. That chesty cough, again, deafened her. Dash, this was important. Where would she train if the Ghost House was sold?

Now a child: 'Pa ... we ... live ... big house? Ooooh ...'

'A rambling building ... but ... can ... be done ...' It was the gruff voice.

Gross, this crouching pose was squashing her organs. Dare she move? No, a creaking trunk was a sure giveaway.

The thin voice: 'Interest rates ... rising ...'

To the sun, Sierra hoped, thinking it might deter him from buying the house because when interest rates shot high, her dad complained that paying off their home was too costly. Seriously, why did this fellow have such a puny tone?

Laughs.

Oh, great, how was she going to hear anything? Well, what really mattered was that the talks, coughs and laughs kept the men from noticing her book. But the musty air inside the trunk was flowing into her nostrils, and though she managed to hold down the sniffles, she could feel a sneeze coming.

'Aaaaa – ch –' Sierra pressed her nose with her hand to snip the second half of that sneeze. Had they heard her? She pricked up her ears. The voices were growing faint but, half-expecting them to return to investigate the noise, she remained as she was. Then as the silence screamed at her, she threw back the lid and climbed out of the trunk to a waft of safety.

She gaped at the spot where the ballet book had fallen.

The book wasn't there.

She looked this way and that.

Still, no book.

Blast! This couldn't be happening. It couldn't.

Sierra shed her momentary daze and raced to the door, punching her forehead with her fist. Had the agent taken it? Or was it the father? Or the kid? But, but how was it that they hadn't said a word about it? She wouldn't have missed something like that. To the front of the house, she belted along the hallway despite the rackety floorboards.

The rumpus didn't matter because everyone had gone.

So had the ballet book.

And so had Rosella.

Chapter 13

Sierra wound her arms around her head. It wasn't about her training coming to an end; she could sense something much bigger, much graver, more sinister.

Rosella could be in danger now.

She thrashed along Fern Grove, her heart pounding. The kid. The kid. It had to be the kid. The kid, who had sounded like a girl, could be the only one to bag the book but say nothing, possibly fearing that the adults wouldn't let her have it. Besides, how would that weeny-voiced father notice she'd got it when he was *busy* eyeing Sierra's training ground? And if it had been the agent, wouldn't he have mentioned it or given the place a walkover, rather than scampering off as he did?

'I'm on my way, Rosella,' she cried, tearing down Pebbleridge Road. She'd tell the agent at Craig Properties that the ballet book was hers even if it got her into trouble for being there. *She didn't care!* Not any longer. Wasn't Rosella's plight more precarious than hers? What if that child let Rosella disappear? She promised she'd never let that happen. She promised. She promised.

She had to rescue Rosella.

When Sierra got to Craig Properties, she grabbed the handle of the glass sliding door. That's when she saw the board that hung in front of her nose.

Closed.

She glared at her watch. It was 5 o'clock already. She had to get her claws on the book before that kid or someone else discovered Rosella inside it. But by after school *tomorrow* ... Her mouth crowded with what tasted like milk well past its sell-by-date. She swallowed to get rid of it and turned to leave, yet couldn't.

Suppose the agent saw the book later and got it away from the child? The book could be in here.

And Rosella!

Sierra peeped through the door, and her eyes followed a row of black plastic chairs which led to a tall matching counter, with a bell fixed at one end and a rack of business cards at the other. No evidence of the ballet book. That sour taste made her swallow again.

Would tomorrow be too late?

∞

When Sierra got home, her grandma called out to her. Letting the bag on her shoulders slide to the floor, she zipped into the kitchen. 'Grandma, are you all right?'

'Mum brought me home and then took Rory for swimming, and I'm fine, dear.' In spite of what she said, her hand shook as she set her mug on the dresser. 'It was my fault. Should never have left that book at Reads –'

'I know how you injured your ankle, Grandma. Rosella told me.' Sierra rubbed her watery eyes. 'But I lost the book, I lost it!'

'*Lost it?*'

'Rosella was training me as well, but I don't care about the audition or, or that surreal dancer, Kim, any more. What's dire is that the book might have fallen into the wrong hands. And with that spooky two-hour deadline tying Rosella to the book, she can't get away, c-can she?' Sierra buried her face in her grandma's frail shoulder, which somehow felt pillowy, and wept.

'Hush, dear. Hush, hush.' Her grandma patted her on the back. 'How did you lose the book?' she asked, when Sierra's crying had reduced to sniffles.

Sierra explained how it happened, omitting the bit about her visit to Craig Properties. She didn't want her grandma to smell trouble and talk her out of going there the next day.

Her grandma placed her palms together. 'We have to pray for Rosella's safety – praying is all we can do now.'

Yet Sierra could hear *unknowns* banging inside her, and realised it would go on until she filled the remaining gaps in the puzzle. 'Tell me everything, Grandma, I want to know everything,' she said.

Her grandma dropped into a chair at the dining table as if her feet wouldn't be able to hold up the weight of her tale. 'Well, dear, I got the book when I was twelve, and then stumbled upon the dancer inside.' Again that faraway look occupied her eyes. 'She trained me, yes, daily. I thought I was the luckiest girl in the world, till I had the injury.'

Sierra joined her at the table. 'Rosella told me you didn't open the book after that,' she said, hoping it would lead to the parts of the mystery she couldn't quite put her finger on.

Her grandma fiddled with the beads round her neck.

'But why?' Sierra probed. 'Why didn't you speak to her?'

'I was angry – angry with the whole world but especially with Rosella.'

'That's not fair, Grandma!'

'Yes, dear, but anger blinds one.'

'So for years Rosella didn't get to dance,' Sierra said hotly.

Her grandma kept on gripping her beads until her knuckles bulged. 'I don't know what got into me! Yet I didn't tell my parents that I got injured when Rosella was training me. They would have taken the book, and there was no telling what would have become of her.'

'Thanks, Grandma.' An itsy fraction of Sierra's heart forgave her for depriving Rosella of her dancing. 'Then Mum and Aunt Kelly?'

'Told them the same – that it happened while I was practising on my own.'

Sierra nudged her chair closer to the table, expecting to pounce on a big bit of the unknown. 'What made you leave the book for sale?'

'The anniversary of my accident.' Her grandma clasped her hands and then unclasped them. 'I battle through that day each year. This year, I ultimately faced what I'd done. I'd punished Rosella for something that wasn't her fault! I wanted to make it up to her. But the complication wasn't just that those spells couldn't be broken by anyone else, was it? The risk of trying to get her out of the book once and for all –'

'Yup, the witch's threat to make her *disappear*,' Sierra said, nodding. 'Wasn't that the one thing Rosella was afraid of? Even when I asked her whether that mistake the witch made in her *no-way-out* spell might have created a means of escape – a sort of loophole – she panicked.'

Her grandma wrung her hands. 'And so, I didn't want to gamble when I'd *already* caused her grief. The least I could do was to give her the opportunity to dance again. But I couldn't bear to open the book myself. Selling it seemed –'

'That was risky too! What if the person who bought it was nasty to Rosella and, and neglectful?'

'Of course, I felt anxious, dear. Nevertheless, I thought that Rosella wouldn't be in harm's way because only a ballet lover would buy a book like that. When I went to Kelly's for her birthday, I left it at Reads.' Her grandma's eyes looked haunted. 'But since then I've had sleepless nights, wondering whether Rosella is okay.'

Sierra arched a brow. 'Why Reads? Aren't there second-hand bookshops in Bellmeadows?'

Drops of sweat surfaced on her grandma's forehead. 'It would have been dicey.'

'Dicey?'

'Urm ... the witch ...' Her grandma drew a pattern on the table with her finger. 'Er, Azra. She also lives in Bellmeadows.'

'*In Bellmeadows?*' Sierra bounced off her chair, only to fall back. 'Do you know the house?'

'No, except that she lives down Tittle Street. That's, er, two streets from Cherry Street.'

'*Two streets from you?*' Sierra's insides shrank. She thumped on the table. 'I hate her! I hate her!'

Her grandma leaned forward and covered Sierra's fist with her hand, and said, 'Little did I know that the next owner of *The Ballerina's Treasure Trove* would be my granddaughter.'

'And *the secret of the ballet book* passed on to me.' The banging inside Sierra stopped. 'Then Rosella trained me, just as she trained you – so your secret became my secret!'

Chapter 14

After school the next day, hovering outside their class Sierra found Kim.

'Got a minute?' Kim asked.

'Have to dash,' Sierra said, hoping Kim couldn't hear her mind going, *Craig Properties, Craig Properties, Craig Properties ...*

'Racing off again!' Kim whined.

'Not always.'

'Yah, seen you rev after school. To practise, right?'

'Practise?'

'Thought you might be going to the dance centre. At my last ballet school it was real cool. Students were allowed to use the studios if there were no classes going on.'

'It's the exams,' Sierra said. 'Scholarship holders have to maintain their grades.'

'Oh, those exams.'

Craig Properties, Craig Properties, Craig Properties ...

Kim switched on her sugary smile and again its sweetness extended to her voice. 'Hey, can I borrow *The Ballerina's Treasure* book for a teeny-tiny week? Fed up of doing the same old exercises.'

'I'm ploughing through it,' Sierra said. Seriously, when was Miss *Perfect* going to relinquish nosing around?

A look of doubt swept across Kim's face. 'Is the book that long?'

'With the swotting, I don't have much time,' Sierra said, hopelessly trying to stop her right foot tapping the ground.

Kim got the giggles. 'Aren't you restless! You're not wangling extra ballet classes, right?'

'You're kidding!' Sierra cringed at how close Kim was to her secret. She'd need lenses behind her head if she got the book back. Yet she pointed her nose at the sky. She wasn't going to rupture because of the needle-sharp glint in Kim's eyes.

'No need to get uptight, I just asked because you're a swell dancer,' Kim said, her tone somehow free of its added-sugar flavour.

Still, Sierra strode through the quadrangle to shake off the itchy unease that beset her whenever she was around Kim, and when she saw the black iron gates she almost ran.

∞

Sierra peeped through the gaps between the wooden screens that were mounted with pictures of houses and set beside the windows of Craig Properties. What she saw was a mass of crinkly caramel hair behind the black counter. Wishing she had a quick-fix for the nervy fizzes in her stomach, she entered the office.

The caramel head smiled broadly. 'How may I help you?'

'Er, the large house at Fern Grove,' Sierra said. 'Could ... could I see the agent in charge?'

'A moment.' The lady's smile didn't shrink.

That was easy, Sierra thought, glad that she had reacted as if it was common for children to walk in for details on houses.

The lady opened the door behind her, knocking softly. 'Mr Fairweather, there's, urm, a person here enquiring about the Fern Grove house.'

The agent was out in a flash. When he saw Sierra, his eyes narrowed down to slits.

Sierra's mouth went dry. 'Er, er, I was r-reading there last evening,' she stuttered. 'And, and I lost, er, mis-misplaced my book.'

'You were at the house?'

That *gruff* voice.

Mr Fairweather wobbled his thick eyebrows. 'How did you get inside?'

'I didn't. I was only on the veranda.'

'The book must be a bestseller for you to come searching for it!' The agent tugged his bushy beard. 'What's it called?'

He hasn't seen it! 'It's a ballet book,' Sierra said, now decided more than ever that the book was with the kid. 'Er, and I was wondering whether the … the child who came there with her f-father, took it.'

'The child? Oh, so you were there when we arrived and went into hiding when you saw us!' Mr Fairweather's face was stony. 'What made you think you could use an empty house as your hideout, or should I say *readout*? Trespassing is a serious offence. I should let your parents know what you get up to after school.'

'Don't!' Sierra said. 'I meant no harm, and it won't happen again.'

'It certainly won't! Mind if I catch you anywhere there again, there'll be trouble. Off with you, before I *do* ring your parents. Got a meeting to get to.'

Sierra's heart bottomed. 'But, but the book?'

Mr Fairweather glanced at the lady and grunted. 'Weren't they in a mighty hurry to see the place? Barely got the *Sale* board fixed!'

'I could collect the book from them myself if –' Sierra began.

Mr Fairweather boxed on as though she wasn't there. 'Wasted my time. Opted for another property, it *seems*.' He snorted. 'Ghosts! My foot!'

The lady made a range of clicking sounds.

Sierra got it at once, oh, yes; the buyer would have heard the rumours about the Ghost House and chickened out. What rotten luck. She couldn't let it end like this.

However, it looked as though she was being dismissed. Mr Fairweather was picking some business cards from the counter and stuffing them into his white shirt pocket.

'But don't you have their address, or anything, on your computer?' Sierra persevered, hoping her voice wasn't transmitting distress signals.

As if to soothe his patience, the agent stroked the bald patch at the front of his head. 'Deleted! Gone! Understood?'

Sierra's brain rattled inside her to confirm she had.

No address.

No ballet book.

No Rosella.

Sierra scarpered from Craig Properties. She stared at Pebbleridge Road as if a new town had been born; nothing felt normal. Her heart was in shreds, and she wished she could shred her brain too because it couldn't put her on a route to bail Rosella, short of a miracle.

Lost Rosella ... lost ... lost ... lost ... her mind tormented her till she nearly threw up. She leaned on the wall next to the sliding door of the office, getting sicker by the minute.

What was she to do?

Oops. It was getting a little crowded. Sierra shifted further from the door. Wallowing in her misery, she hadn't seen this woman or this Goldilocks-looking girl walking along the road until they were standing right by her, talking.

'Told you to do ballet, Dixie, but you wanted tap. And now you want ballet?'

Sierra's eyes flew to the little girl.

'No, Ma! I want to go on doing tap.' She pouted. 'I don't want this book.'

The woman appeared sceptical. 'You took it for *nothin'*?'

Dixie was hopping from foot to foot with the book under her arm.

'But you can't take away somethin' that's not yours!' The mother's face darkened with irritation. 'Me afternoon gone, and such a lot to get done.' She slid the door of Craig Properties and pointed inside. 'Hurry! Give it back.'

Sierra's eyes were now riveted on the miracle tucked under Dixie's arm.

The Ballerina's Treasure Trove.

Chapter 15

Sierra kept staring as if she was watching a Dance of Miracles. A coincidence like this didn't just happen. Suppose they'd arrived after she left? Things were finally going her way.

Rosella would be with her in a matter of minutes, she reckoned, the anticipation making her giddy. She sucked in a breath, a life-sized one, to hold down the excitement bubbling inside her. Then she crept to the glass sliding door, curling her toes as though she was trying to fit into Dixie's footprints so that she didn't lose the child.

Dixie was skipping across the office, her red frilly frock doing a jig, her mother following her. Mr Fairweather was standing by the counter dangling a bunch of keys, evidently ready to go for his meeting. But they rocked up to him. They were talking to him now.

Sierra slipped in.

Mr Fairweather squinted at her. 'There she is!'

Dixie's mother pivoted on her heels. 'Girlie, I'm sorry me little one carried off your book. She didn't mean no trouble.'

Before Sierra could say a word, Dixie stretched her arms and held the book out under Sierra's nose. She appeared eager to return it. Worried she might change her mind, Sierra snatched it. Then not wanting to be labelled rude, she put up a smile. 'Yay!'

'Like I was sayin', no harm done.' The mother's sunken brown eyes flitted between Sierra and the agent as if she was gauging whether they were going to lay charges against Dixie.

Sierra peeped at the door with the corner of her eye. 'Thank you, Mr Fairweather.'

'Not that fast.' The agent tweaked his beard and showered her with a look of disapproval. 'I'm warning you again – no setting foot in that house!'

'Yes, Mr Fairweather.' Dreading a cross-examination, Sierra fled to the door. She was about to slide it when she felt a tug at her sleeve. Now what? She hardened her grasp on the book and turned reluctantly.

The egg-shaped eyes raised to hers were Dixie's.

'Thought of changing to ballet when I saw the book,' she said sheepishly. 'But I'm not! I'm doing tap.'

'Great!' Sierra said.

'Told her I didn't want to do ballet.'

Sierra's nose twitched. 'Told who? Your mum?'

Dixie began tapping her foot – heel, toe, toe, heel.

'Told *who*?' Sierra prodded, her surroundings oddly smelling fishy.

'The pop-up dancer,' Dixie whispered.

The hairs on the nape of Sierra's neck stood, she felt it. *This kid had flipped to page 33!* Her gravest concern had come true. She stood paralysed, her eyes locking with Dixie.

'She wasn't scary cos she had a smiley face,' Dixie said, though her voice faltered. 'I didn't show her to Ma cos she would have told Ma to make me do ballet. And Ma would have, cos she's a ballet nut.' She skipped off to her mother and latched on to her zebra-striped skirt.

Come back, Dixie, come back, Sierra bawled voicelessly.

'A second, poppet. Ma hasn't finished speakin' to this nice man.' The woman untangled Dixie's hand from her skirt.

Sierra heaved a sigh of relief. At least Dixie's mother wasn't in a hurry any more. *Come back, Dixie, come back.*

And Dixie did. Then she stepped to the left and shuffled her right foot. She stepped to the right and shuffled her left foot. 'Said I do tap.'

Sierra placed her hands on her knees and levelled with Dixie. 'Is the pop-up dancer in the book?'

Dixie seemed puzzled. 'Doesn't she live inside it?' She watched her feet doing something like step-shuffle-hop. Yet soon she stopped, and her mouth hung at an angle. 'When I got home yesterday, Ma put the book away cos it wasn't mine! But today, cos she wanted to bake Grandpa's birthday cake, she let me have it after lunch to read quietly in my room. And that pop-up didn't scare me, not a bit,' she said once more, as though she was having a go at believing it. She eyed the book in Sierra's hand and smiled archly. 'Now she *can't* talk to Ma. If Ma saw –'

'Did you close the book within two hours?' Sierra asked, the witch's deadline making her flinch.

Dixie did a step-shuffle without the hop. Sierra restrained her urge to grab Dixie by the shoulders to get her to stand still.

'Dunno,' Dixie said.

Sierra's breath quickened. 'Was the pop-up dancer there – in your room – until you shut the book?'

'Oooh, yes!' Dixie said, launching into a sequence of jumps.

Sierra's roaring pulse subsided. For an instant she'd imagined that ...

Dixie added some turns to her jumps. Her shiny gold hair frolicked in the air and her voice sounded disjointed. 'The ... room ... got ... clou ... dy ... but ... I ... saw ... blu ... ey ... lips ... and ... and ... sh-she ... was ... whi ... tish.'

'*Whitish?*' *Was Rosella growing pale, disappearing?* Faintish from shock, Sierra's head spun – people, furniture, pictures, pot plants were all whizzing around her, doubling and tripling.

Dixie dropped her jump-turn move. She drew an outline in the air with her finger. It looked like a human being. 'Maybe the pop-up dancer was sick,' she said, her face flushed with bewilderment. 'Cos then, she started fading.'

Sierra's heart leapt into her mouth. *No, oh, Rosellaaaaaaaa!*

'Dixie!'

'Coming, Ma.'

'I like your tap dancing,' Sierra cut in mid-gasp, striving to hold Dixie's attention.

It worked.

Dixie's eyes glistened in spite of her perplexity.

Sierra planted her hands on Dixie's shoulders. *Got her!* She peered into Dixie's face. 'D-did you close the book *before* the pop-up dancer f-faded away?' she stammered.

Dixie seemed confused again. 'Doesn't she live inside the book?'

A torrent of frustration drove Sierra from the office; she wasn't going to get any more out of Dixie. But if Rosella had been fading, she had to have reached her two-hour deadline, Sierra thought, feeling prickly all over. *So if Dixie hadn't shut the book at once for Rosella to go in, she would have disappeared!*

Everything inside Sierra spiralled to the soles of her feet, including her brain. She couldn't think. Should she open the book to see what had happened? No-no, what if Rosella stepped out? She'd have to go home. No, she couldn't, she couldn't – Rory's caught-you-doing-the-soppy-soppy grin was flashing in her mind. Finally, her brain kicked in and thrust her towards the nearest location where nobody would notice. Debster Park.

Now ducking and swerving, Sierra charged through the bustle on Pebbleridge Road. 'Are you in here?' she called repeatedly, holding the book to her heart. Never had she seen the trees, houses and lamp posts on the way looking like blotches of black and grey. The wind was also being awkward, humming a mournful tune. The park, the park, oh, at last. But then, she wanted to hurl herself on the ground and beat her chest because she couldn't open the book there.

In full swing was a fair!

'Fern Grove!' she spluttered, now that it was only two streets from where she was and usually deserted. She raced on hugging the book even closer to her. If Rosella had disappeared wouldn't that mean she was as good as dead? And all because *she* had been irresponsible. *I'm sorry, I'm sorry, I'm sorry,* her mind howled, but those words, showing no mercy, refused to comfort her. A huge tremble inside her shoved her along the pavement. Was she a killer?

A killer ... a killer ... a killer ...

When she got to the lonely stretch of Fern Grove, on the lane were two women having a powwow. Was she *seeing* things today? To remain unnoticed, she slowed to a snail pace which made each step feel like torture. Worse, she couldn't turn to the page down this road either.

Er, but wasn't Mr Fairweather going to be tucked away at a meeting? What she needed was a moment inside the Ghost House. An itty-bitty moment.

Sierra crashed on the floor of the ballroom and opened the book. She was about to learn Rosella's fate. All of a sudden, she was petrified of the shadow that formed on page 33 whenever Rosella came out as it indicated that she was not in the book. Therefore if that dark human-shaped figure was still there ...

Sierra's chest tightened. She was almost glad that her clammy fingers were getting stuck to the pages and making them difficult to flick. Yet unwilling to lose hope, she rubbed that figure from her mind and filled it with the picture of Rosella. Oh, how she wanted to cling to that image because it was as though the shadow had turned back into the picture which could only happen if Rosella had entered the closing book. But what would Sierra see on the *page*?

The picture of Rosella?
Or
The shadow?

Chapter 16

'*Rosella!*'

The joy in Sierra's heart nearly lifted her off the ground. *Dixie, you did it!* Had she freaked out when she saw Rosella fading and slapped the book shut? Or had she been given instructions on closing the book and the guilt from not following them put her into action?

The hard cold floor – Sierra felt it again. Would Rosella arise from the picture as on other days? What if the *disappearing* Rosella was too frail? Was somehow different?

Not blinking, not breathing, she watched the page.

The picture was shivering as it usually did.

Now abating as it usually did ...

She held her breath. Would it turn into ...?

'*Yes!*'

The shadow ... wavering ... becoming more intense ...

Oh, please ... Was that the outline of a person forming?

'*Yeeeees!*' Sierra sprang to her feet. 'Be the same,' she said, vowing she'd set aside her other wishes if this one was granted.

Rosella appeared.

Sierra covered her mouth with her hands.

Rosella's arms looked as if they were floating.

She was doing a port de bras *sequence!*

Laughing and crying at the same time, Sierra flung herself at Rosella. 'You came! You came!'

'Don't I always? What's brought *this* on?'

'And you *are* the same.'

'Why wouldn't I be?' Rosella grinned, apparently shrugging away the wonderment that had crept into her eyes. 'Thought I might have had a hair-cut?'

'But, but Dixie said –'

'*Dixie?*'

'The girl –'

'There was a girl here?' Rosella asked, even tilting her head the way she often did.

Why was Rosella talking as though she'd never met Dixie? Sierra pressed her lips together afraid to say more until she could fathom Rosella's bizarre behaviour.

Rosella was quizzical. 'You mean a girl-ghost? Didn't we establish that there were no ghosts here? Not sure I believe in them.' Her eyes were now teasing. 'Come on, scaredy-cat! Stop staring at me as if *I* was a ghost. With the audition drawing close, I thought we should focus today on all types of sequences. You'll be able to pick up whatever they dole out. But first things first, I'll race you to the *barre*.'

Sierra recoiled in alarm. Plainly, Rosella had no recollection of Dixie. None whatsoever. Could her time with Dixie have been erased from her memory because she was weak enough to fade when she went into the book? The more Sierra considered it, the likelier it seemed.

She cleared her throat to tell Rosella everything and then bit back the words, her mind racing. If Rosella learned she had almost disappeared, she'd live imagining it could happen again. 'Er, this house is for sale,' Sierra said. 'We can't use it any longer, came here to explain.'

'Oh, it was the lady overseeing the sale you were referring to.'

'Urm, I also feel a bit feverish,' Sierra said, anxious to make the *girl* topic go away.

'Then we'd better get you well first, before worrying about another place for training.' Rosella reached for her.

But Sierra didn't sense Rosella's palm on her forehead or neck because she'd gone numb from top to toe. Suppose Rosella's entire life had been wiped from her memory? Suppose she had remained fragile and unable to dance again? Suppose she *had* disappeared?

Right then and there Sierra made a decision.

She had to get Rosella out of *The Ballerina's Treasure Trove* for good.

Chapter 17

The last two schooldays had been a nail-biting countdown. It was Saturday morning at last, and Sierra and her grandma were on the bus to Cherry Street.

Sierra glanced at her grandma sitting stiffly beside her. 'It will be okay, Grandma.'

Her grandma began fidgeting with the rings on her fingers. 'I hope we are doing the right thing, dear.'

'Well,' Sierra said earnestly, 'after what happened with Dixie, I think Rosella is at risk even if she lives on the page. She almost disappeared, didn't she?'

'You're correct, dear. I'm sure you're correct. We have to get Rosella out of the book.'

Sierra wasn't surprised that her grandma was fraught, knowing she was against doing what might aggravate Rosella's predicament. 'Grandma, if you'd rather not, I could go on my own.'

'Of course not.' A wave of remorse washed over her grandma's face. 'This could be my opening to do something for Rosella. Show her how sorry I am.'

'I'm spooked too, Grandma. Really spooked. But as you said, with those nobody-else-can-break spells and Azra's will-make-you-disappear-if-you-get-out threat, I couldn't come up with a rescue package either, despite sweating about it all term! *This* is the only way to save Rosella, although I couldn't bring myself to open the book to tell her what we were going to do. She'd have a panic attack if she knew.' Sierra peeked at *The Ballerina's Treasure Trove* inside the canvas bag on her lap as if she was pleading with Rosella to trust her.

'I *have* to ask Azra to break her spells,' she pressed on. 'We have no choice. But the good part about it is if that witch breaks them herself, she won't feel cheated.

Then she wouldn't have cause to go ahead with her threat. Yup? And isn't that how Rosella can be truly free?'

'Yes, dear, but what if Azra refuses?' Her grandma's voice was tense.

A shiver jetted through Sierra's spine. 'The downside will be that Rosella remains in the book, Grandma. As long as she stays there Azra won't make her disappear.'

Her grandma blinked rapidly. 'A witch who casts spells that no one else can undo must be all-powerful.'

'She must also be a ratbag who should be shooed from this planet! But we still have to face her. We can't let the horrible things that could happen get to us.' Sierra sat upright in her seat as though being taller might give her the mettle to stick to her plan in spite of the dangers. 'Think of it, Grandma! Azra is bound to be stunned when Rosella comes out of the book, because she doesn't know she omitted page 33 in the *no-way-out* spell. Just as I'd hoped all along, now we can actually turn that mistake to our advantage. Yup, that's right, by using her flustered state to have her believe that her what's-it-called spells are *wearing out*. It, it will shatter her invincible status, make her vulnerable, more like a human being. And that might help us to get through to her, Grandma, and persuade her to let Rosella go.'

Her grandma stopped tinkering with her rings, and her eyes were peppered with optimism. 'Positive thinking,' she said.

Sierra gave her grandma's hand a squeeze.

∞

When the bus halted at Cherry Street, they hopped off. 'Two streets from you, didn't you say?' Sierra stared one way and then the other.

'Left, dear.'

They soldiered on until they were at the top of Tittle Street.

Sierra surveyed the narrow road, her skin crawling. 'Okay, we don't know the number of Azra's home. But if we locate the blue cottage Rosella told me she lived in, we would have reduced our search to two houses. The one on the left or right.'

Her grandma shifted from foot to foot. 'The cottage might not be blue now, it could have been repainted.'

'Watching out for a blue house for starters won't hurt,' Sierra insisted, even while admitting to herself that her grandma was probably correct. 'If we don't spot one, we'll have to go from door to door asking for Azra, I suppose.'

They set off along Tittle Street, Sierra observing the homes on the side they were on and her grandma keeping an eye on those across the street to the right.

Minutes later, no blue cottage and they were reaching the end of the road.

'We'll have to toddle back slower so as not to miss anything,' her grandma said.

But Sierra was waving her finger at the house she had got up to. The walls weren't blue.

The window frames and the front door were.

'That could be where Rosella lived!' A flare of hope grabbed Sierra, while not daring to think it might be the case. 'The current owners may have painted the walls but left the frames and door as they were.' She scuttled to the gate for a better view and then felt doubtful about her theory. 'If those frames were old, shouldn't the blue paint be flaking or something?'

Her grandma joined her. 'Hmm, they could have been redone, but these people might have used the original colour. They may have wanted to maintain the old style, and this may be how the cottage was.'

'Yup, possible, because blue is not a colour commonly used for frames. This could be what Rosella was referring to.' Sierra studied the homes on both sides. 'The house on the left is odd,' she said. 'See how all the blinds are down as if they don't want anyone to peep? It might be the best place to start the door-knocking.'

So they trod up the pebbly path to the door. Before they could catch their breaths, it opened.

Sierra bit her lip in disappointment. The woman towering over them didn't look like an old witch who'd been around *forever*. With a willowy figure and ginger hair that fell to her waist in waves, she was almost beautiful in spite of her crooked nose.

However ...

Sierra went icy-cold.

Her grandma clutched convulsively at her arm. Was she sensing the same dark vibes that made Sierra freeze?

Then could this person somehow be ... 'Azra?' Sierra blurted.

The woman scratched her pointy chin and examined their faces as though she was fishing for clues. 'What do you want?'

Sierra stood electrified by the current that was ripping through her body. *It was the witch!* 'Er, it's about, er –'

Azra gave Sierra's grandma a sidelong glance.

'Spells.' Her grandma sounded as if the word had been raked from her mouth.

Azra's facial muscles tightened, unease overtaking her curiosity. 'Know nothing,' she said, and retreated, pulling the door after her.

Sierra lunged at the closing door; they couldn't let her turn tail, not now. 'The spells you put on Rosella,' she called.

Azra popped her head out. Sierra inched back, certain she'd seen Azra's steel-grey pupils become yellow and then orange for a nanosecond. Was she magically scanning her list of victims to detect Rosella?

Next, Azra held the door open and let them in.

Sierra thrust herself forward as her body was pulling away and, with her grandma, followed the witch to a room. She crept in dreading she'd trip on bottles of potions or fall into a bubbling cauldron. With the exception of an antique desk, though, the place was similar to other living rooms she had seen. Perhaps witches who lived among regular folk hid their witchy devices to avoid being hunted down, she figured. Didn't Rosella tell her that Azra generally abstained from casting spells around where she lived? Despite the normality, Sierra trembled inside her skin.

What if the witch put *them* in a book?

Made *them* disappear?

Her brain pegged on: *what if, what if, what if?*

But it was too late to turn back.

Positive thinking, Sierra hissed silently, to block the *what ifs*. Then, mustering the courage, she said, 'Rosella has been living inside the book you put her into for f-far too long. We've, er, come here to ask you to – to find it in your heart to b-break your spells.'

'Hah?' Azra hooted. 'Expect me to believe you spoke to a character in a book?'

'She's real, and you know you put her in there,' Sierra's grandma said.

'But she was able to tell us everything,' Sierra added, 'because she comes out –'

'*Comes out?* Bah! Impossible.' Azra's gingery waves straightened for a moment and lifted off her shoulders. From the deep pocket in her long, midnight blue gown, she dredged up a sizeable key. Then she unlocked the desk drawer and produced a book bound in leather.

It was a book of spells.

'*Extremico Evilius*,' she declared, laying it on the desk.

'Must be the *Ex*-something spells Rosella was on about,' Sierra mumbled to her grandma.

'Worst-of-the-worst is what that stands for!'Azra said. 'For others to break these spells, they have to meet *rules* which are beyond them.' She rubbed her hands in evil delight. 'Get what that means? Only I can break them!'

Bad move: appealing to a wicked witch didn't work. It was time to execute her plan. Sierra's stomach did a somersault. Who could bring down one as formidable as Azra? Easier said than done. 'Nobody broke your spells,' she croaked. 'They're just wearing –' She jammed her mouth.

That gaze.

Azra's pupils were yellow again, and switching to orange.

They were focused on the sling-bag on Sierra's shoulder.

Before Sierra knew what was happening, *The Ballerina's Treasure Trove* inside her bag was in Azra's hands.

It was turned to page 33.

And Rosella was standing in front of Azra.

The witch dashed the ballet book on the floor, and then flung her arms above her head and shot fire balls at the ceiling. 'So it's true!'

'*Those eyes!*' Gasping, Rosella took a step back and another and another. She cowered as though terror was biting her.

'You've been dabbling with my spells,'Azra said.

'I d-didn't. You made a mistake.'

Oh, no, Rosella, you shouldn't have told her it was a mistake. Now we can't make her feel she's losing it!

Sierra darted up to Rosella and gave her a keep-your-lips-sealed look. In return, Rosella stared at her blankly, showing no signs of recognising her. Sierra shuddered. Was this also Azra's bewitching? This meant she couldn't even caution Rosella.

Azra cackled, making Sierra's eardrums flap. 'Mistake, hah? Think I'm a witch-brat-in-training?'

Rosella's voice quaked. 'I h-heard you casting a *live-in* spell to p-put me into page 33. B-but you didn't repeat that number when you ch-chanted the other page numbers for your *no-way-out* spell – see why th-that spell isn't attached to p-page 33?'

Rosella, you've blown our plan!

'I've been casting spells for a century!' Azra raved.

Liar, Sierra thought. Looking like that, how could she even be that age?

'Mistake. Bah!' Azra spat. 'But nobody has ever softened up an *Extremico Evilius* spell.'

'It could be wearing out,' Sierra threw in, grasping the opportunity to make the witch feel unarmed.

But Azra cackled once more. '*Extremico Evilius* spells don't wear out like other spells! The rule says, "life-time".'

'*Rules!*' Sierra almost choked on the word. She hadn't realised there were rules, especially one with a life-time guarantee. It explained why Azra appeared almighty, instead of waning. Fear stomped through Sierra's body, crushing her to bits. Now it wouldn't be too long before the witch made them *all* disappear.

How could she have led them to this!

'You're a danger to witchcraft!' Azra said, storming over to Rosella.

Rosella staggered backwards. 'I didn't interfere with your spells. Didn't!'

'You know what I'm going to do?' Azra gazed at the spell book with her yellowing pupils and it flipped to the page she seemingly wanted. She seized Rosella with those eyes and said, 'With this spell you shall disappear.'

'*Nooooo!*' Rosella shrieked, holding her hands in front of her face. Then she spun on her heels and fled to the door.

Azra eyed the lock.

It clicked.

Seeing Rosella yanking the door which was refusing to budge, Sierra flew to the window. She pushed up the blind and gasped.

Fixed to that window was an iron grille she was sure she hadn't seen from outside the house.

No use.

There was no way out.

Then Azra zoomed in on Rosella again with pupils now orange. 'Zanikar disashi statet askooma nashmere ...'

In horror, Sierra and her grandma gaped at Rosella.

A thick dark cloud had formed around her.

Rosella was turning white.

Chapter 18

'I *won't* ruin her life once more!' Sierra's grandma pushed her way up to Azra. 'Set Rosella free and make me disappear!'

Azra's pupils instantly altered; they looked like blobs of blood.

'*Grandmaaaaaaa!*' Sierra leapt in front of her. Appalled, she turned beseeching eyes on Azra, saying the first thing that came to her head. 'Make *me* disappear, and let them both go!'

'*Don't!*' Her grandma shoved her away from the witch. 'Rosella and you have dreams, let Azra take me!'

To get again to Azra, with a mammoth gulp of air, Sierra threw a leg forward, but stopped short.

Azra's pupils weren't red any more.

Nor were they orange or yellow.

They were back to their natural colour, grey.

'You agitated the spell!' Azra shrieked. Then, wailing, into a chair she collapsed.

There was a clap of thunder, and the house shook.

Sierra screamed, glancing over her shoulder.

The spell book had fallen on to the floor.

The locked door had burst open.

And Rosella had regained her rosy appearance.

'The spell didn't work, thank goodness!' Sierra said, pelting towards her.

But Rosella was sliding across the floor as if an unseen force was drawing her. She was heading towards the light now pulsing from the open page of the spell book.

She picked it and pored over the page, and then turned to Sierra with that distant look lifted from her eyes. 'This page is about agitated spells,' she said.

Sierra and her grandma rushed to her.

'The page is blank,' Sierra said. Oh, no. It was Rosella's memory last time; this time was she going weird?

'*Rules that agitate Extremico Evilius spells,*' Rosella read.

Sierra and her grandma exchanged glances.

'Perhaps only she is allowed to *see* the rules,' her grandma whispered, 'as she's the one under the *Extreme*-whatever spells.'

Azra raised her head. 'W-wasn't afraid to cast *Extremico Evilius* spells ... wasn't afraid ... no, no ... because I didn't think anyone would ag-agitate –' Her chin sank into her chest.

'The writing on the page is getting fainter,' Rosella cried.

'Read it quick!' Sierra said, looking doubtfully at her grandma.

Rosella sped through the page of rules:

'*A person offering to sacrifice his or her life on behalf of a victim breaks all the Extremico Evilius spells a witch has cast on that victim.*

'*A second person offering to sacrifice his or her life on behalf of the same victim amounts to a double sacrifice, and therefore it reverses the spells cast on the victim. Henceforth, the witch who cast the spells is now victim to those very spells. To enable these reversals, the witch is converted to a non-witch so that she can't break the spells which have reverted to her, or cast more spells on others. In effect, the witch becomes an ordinary individual, devoid of spell-casting powers.*'

'Just about did it! The words have gone, and the page is blank,' Rosella spluttered, dumping the spell book on the desk.

Sierra and her grandma made noises that seemed as though they'd been cramped in their throats from not wanting to interrupt Rosella. Then Sierra and Rosella clasped hands and swung round the room – and there gushed the sounds of euphoria ...

Until –

Sierra's grandma hollered, 'See Azra!'

'My! Oh, my!' Rosella said.

Azra's face had wrinkled and her ginger hair had greyed ...

She lifted her head again. 'Nobody caught on with my forever life because my *look-different* spell gave the impression there were several people living here. My *don't-notice-me* spell deflected too much interest. Now that I can't cast spells, all I can look is ordinary!'

Sierra gasped. *It was a spell that had made the witch appear young!*

After several attempts, Azra rose from her chair. She wasn't as tall as earlier for she was stooping.

'She's ordinary! Ordinary! That must mean that the spells would have not only broken,' Sierra cried, 'but also *reversed*!' She dived at *The Ballerina's Treasure Trove* that lay abandoned on the floor, and shut it.

Rosella stood right where she was, and into the closing book went Azra.

'*You got me my life back! My life back!*' Shaking uncontrollably, Rosella grabbed Sierra in a hug, and it seemed as though they'd be glued together forever. When she finally let go, her eyes and cheeks were all wet.

Sierra had never seen Rosella shed more than a tear.

Here were years of tears.

Yet after a while, Rosella was her smiling self and nodding at Sierra's grandma. 'Jenny,' she said, 'Sierra told me that her grandma had owned the ballet book. But I would have recognised you with those dimples.'

Sierra's grandma dabbed her eyes. 'And you are the same, dear.'

'I can't thank you enough,' Rosella said, hugging her too.

'*Thank me?* I hope you can forgive a stubborn fool.'

'I get to be eighteen, don't I?'

Wow, was that *forgiveness* or what? Sierra felt the blood rush to her cheeks. It wasn't just Rosella's wisdom, courage or composure that never ceased to astound her. Rosella offered kindness, friendship and forgiveness making her a giver – in spite of everything that had been taken from her. Rosella's values, Sierra realised had taught her far more than ballet. Far more.

Rosella's smiles now slipped away leading in a web of worry that netted her face. 'How can we be certain that Azra is actually in the book?'

'Let's check page 33,' Sierra said.

'What if she has become a witch again?' her grandma asked.

Sierra caved into a tremble. 'But, but she went in as an ordinary person.'

'You're right, Sierra. The answer is in the picture,' Rosella said.

Sierra ducked down to the ballet book and flicked to the page.

Staring at them from the picture was Azra.

The Azra with the wrinkles and greys.

A round of relief-sighs cut through the silence.

But now the picture was moving.

'Close the book!' Sierra's grandma said. 'If allowed out, she might change into a witch.'

'Well then, we've got to test that possibility – how else can we put our minds to rest?' Despite her brave words, Sierra couldn't curb the tremor in her voice. 'If things get ugly, I'll shut the book to send her in,' she said.

Azra tottered from the page, leaving a shadow as Rosella had done.

She didn't turn into a witch.

She scooped up *The Ballerina's Treasure Trove* and tore page 33.

Rosella yelped.

'Not clever!' Sierra yelled. 'You've torn the page with the *live-in* spell so that you won't go into the book. But did you forget that if you don't, you will disappear in two hours?'

'Exactly what I want,' Azra said, flopping into an armchair. 'Now I'm a powerless hag. Powerless, bah! Why would I want to live on in a book, hah?'

The thought of a vanishing act made Sierra's stomach growl as if she'd starved for a week. She wanted to dash off, but the fact that Azra wasn't a witch any longer tugged at her conscience. 'Should we at least wait around till she disappears?' she whispered cautiously, not knowing how Rosella would react.

There seemed no boundary to Rosella's compassion.

'Azra did this to herself, but we must stay,' she said, and settled into a straight-back chair. 'Evil doesn't cure evil.'

Sierra huddled on the two-seater sofa with her grandma, consulting her watch every few minutes. Would Azra display all the symptoms Dixie had seen in Rosella?

A minute to go and nothing had happened.

Sierra shifted to the edge of her seat, wiping her sweaty palms on her jeans. Her eyes were piercing Azra.

Then there was fog.

Azra was becoming peaky ... whitish ...

But Sierra's grandma wasn't pointing at her; she was pointing at the straight-back chair.

'Rosella is also growing pale!' she exclaimed.

Azra stirred in her armchair. 'There might have been a hitch in the spell-breaking process,' she said. 'It's rare, but the disappearing spell is a tough one to break … tougher than the other spells … so … Rosella might still be under that spell … could be why she is – '

'Bluey lips!' Sierra squealed, using Dixie's words. 'They've got – '

'If the reversal of the disappearing spell … works …' Azra's tone was squeaky.

Oh, please, oh, please, don't let her voice die on us before she tells us what's going on! Sierra jumped off the sofa and leaned over her to listen.

'Urm … yes … if the reversal takes place as it should, then, of course, what happens to Rosella will be the opposite of what happens to me. If I get worse, Rosella has to get better …' Azra was barely muttering. 'Say that I … go on getting lighter … then … the colour must return to Rosella. We … we can't both disapp …'

Azra was fading.

'*Rosella?*' Sierra swirled.

Rosella was turning pinkish.

'She's coming back to us!' Sierra's grandma said. 'The disappearing spell is reversing.'

Sierra puffed with glee even as she twisted around to assess Azra. Whoops, what a good thing they'd been compassionate; what if they had left? In their moment of panic, it had been Azra's explanations that had kept them hanging in there. Sierra had a hunch that Azra knew that. Maybe losing her invincibility *did* bring up some heart in her.

Paler … paler … Azra was an outline.

Now the armchair was empty.

Chapter 19

Sierra woke to a phone call on the Saturday morning of her audition.

It was Rosella.

'I'm enjoying Jenny's mothering,' she said. 'Kind of her to say I could stay with her as long as I wanted.'

'Goody! Glad you're going to stick around. Friends always!'

'*Always*,' Rosella confirmed heartily. 'You know what? Last evening, Jenny tipped out the old ballet stuff she'd saved in that suitcase.'

'Oh, great. Looks as if she's come to terms with what happened to her.' Into a bin too went the huge worry Sierra had carried in her heart, and it made her feel light. 'Any plans?'

Rosella chortled. 'What a lot of modern things to get used to! It's a bit awkward as well because I have no formal documentation pertaining to myself. But Jenny is going to take me to a lawyer to see what can be done. After that, think I might start with ballet classes! It might help me to get back to teacher training in one form or the other. Then, thanks to you, I'll be able to follow my dream from the *outside*.'

'Neat!'

'Today, Sierra Ballerina,' Rosella said, now with a serious note tucked into her voice, 'you will begin *your* dream.'

'Thanks to you too, I'm all prepared for the audition,' Sierra said. Was she really hearing herself? It was as though that page Rosella had emerged from for the last time had also supplied a new Sierra.

∞

In the afternoon, after a lot of deliberation, Sierra put on her red roll-up sweatpants and her stripy orange hoodie, and twirled in front of the mirror. Bang on to match her fiery confidence. She poked her head into her parents' bedroom to say goodbye to her dad, in bed with the flu, but he was dozing. No, she couldn't bear to wake him. *Bye Dad*, she thought. *I'm going to come home a winner!*

She nipped down to the family room to collect her almost-cerise-to-match-my-leotard dance bag her grandma had bought her for the audition because it was large enough to house every contingency. Instead of her bag lying on the sofa where she'd left it, she found Rory sprawled there with his nose in a Superman comic.

She *so* didn't have time for this. 'Where's my bag?' she demanded.

Rory undug his nose from the book and his lips shaped into his goofy grin. 'Going for the soppy-soppy?'

Hands on waist she glared at him. She couldn't even call on her dad to referee this. Seriously. Was this the time for practical jokes? But before she could open her mouth to *inform* him that it wasn't, Rory swallowed his smile and wagged his finger at the ground where the stool usually was. Sierra pounced on her dance bag and then shot out knowing better than to get into it with him now. Oh, wasn't he going to cop it later.

She skittered along Pebbleridge Road. This was it: *curtain up* ... the moment to showcase her dancing. The moment when her training had to come together.

And, of course, she had to believe in herself – believe she was talented enough to make her mum realise that her daughter should go on doing ballet. After all, according to her book on Margot Fonteyn, the ballerina got where she got by setting her mind on becoming the world's second best dancer, on learning that Anna Pavlova was the greatest.

With exams done, Sierra had been practising most of her waking hours. *Surely she could pull it off!*

∞

The changing room at the dance centre was buzzing with nervous chatter and laughter. Sierra popped her dance bag on a bench and clapped eyes on Kim doing a few stretches. Surreptitiously, she reviewed Kim's face this time for spots, if not bumps, that could put her in quarantine. No luck, she looked flawless as on other days.

Sierra took her gaze to another place, not wanting her *winner* mood to fizzle away. Then she marched up the passage to read the noticeboard. Yup, they were on at 3 o'clock before the boys' audition. It was obvious that the others around her were as much on edge as she was. All hoping to be soloists at the concert, a few openly acknowledging they wanted to be Princess Aurora or that they'd set their sights on the national competition.

She glanced at the wall clock. It was time to get ready.

Back in the changing room, she began unpacking her things. Leotard, tights, ballet shoes ... shoes. She pawed through her gear for her cloth bag of shoes.

Where was it? Her heart throbbed.

Out came the rest: leg warmers, cardigan, towel, deodorant, hairspray ... She peeked into her dance bag. Comb, headbands, titbits. *Can't be.* She clearly recalled putting in her ballet shoes.

Sierra's eyes darted every which way. Benches, shelves – they were strewn with other people's belongings. Panicking, she dashed around the clutter lifting dance bags off the floor to check beneath.

No shoes.

'Has anyone seen my ballet shoes?' she asked. 'I can't audition without them!'

'Oh, didn't you bring them?' Kim's voice was suitably sympathetic with an exaggerated you-poor-thing tone.

But Sierra didn't miss the hopeful gleam in her blackish eyes.

'Think!' Min said, blowing huffily at her fringe. 'Think what you did with them.'

Sierra half-closed her eyes and relived the day. She pictured her dance bag lying in a heap on the family room floor. 'Rory! It's what *Rory* did with them.' Oh, yes, this was his doing. Her heart sagged as if it was loaded with lead. How could Rory do this to her? How pigheaded. She should have known, and maybe inspected her bag, but it hadn't *seemed* rummaged or anything. 'I've got to get home!' she groaned, hurtling to the door, dripping with dread.

'Wait a sec! My mother just left, she might still be in the car park,' Min said. 'She'd give you a ride.'

They sped to the car park, but there was no trace of Mrs Chan or her car.

The time was ticking.

Should she go in again seeking a lift? Nup, the one certain way of getting home was on her feet. So Sierra sprinted along Pebbleridge Road, quarrelling with the threat of tears. Was she running right into a life with no ballet? Was all her training for *nothing*?

Then she had a vision of Miss Lana's punctuality-is-rule-number-one look, and it swamped her head with calculations. Ten minutes home and ten minutes back? Or would it take twelve? Fifteen? Or more?

Oh, no, would she be late?

When Sierra got home, she saw her mum pulling out of the garage with Rory in the car. 'Mum!' she yelled, belting up the driveway.

Her mum slid down the window. 'Get in, quick, we were bringing your ballet shoes.'

Sierra scrambled into the front seat, collecting her bottle of water and bag of shoes. 'Mum, Rory did this. He did it! He did it!' she sobbed.

'We'll address his behaviour tonight,' her mum said, 'but keep calm, sweetie, or you won't be at your best.'

'I didn't do it on p-purpose, I didn't know it was your d-dance bag, it was a different c-colour!' Rory's voice sounded like hiccups. 'I o-opened it to see what was inside. If it was p-private you shouldn't have plonked it on the sofa.'

'That's not your business, it wasn't yours to open!' A drop of guilt splashed on Sierra's rage. True, her old dance bag was navy blue. And perhaps it had been over-eagerness that had coaxed her to take her packed bag downstairs to the family room.

'I dragged it to the ground because I wanted to get on the sofa,' Rory said. 'It toppled and some things f-fell out. I put them in! I didn't see the bottle roll away, or, or that small b-bag. Only Mum saw –'

'You must have been in an awful hurry, Sierra,' her mum said. 'The stool had got thrown back, but I spotted your shoe-bag under it as soon as I walked into the family room to see to Rory. Then I noticed the bottle further along the floor. Not like you to be careless.'

'I was frantic, Mum! When I saw my dance bag, I snatched it and ran. Thought Rory had hidden –'

'I didn't! I wanted space to read.' Rory burst into tears. 'W-won't you be able to do the ballet j-job?'

'*Job?*' Sierra turned and stared at Rory slumped in the back seat. He must have heard her saying that ballet was going to be her job when their mum had prattled on about *proper* jobs.

Rory's lips shook. 'Dad won't have a j-job also.' His tear-stained face looked purple and fear oozed from his eyes.

Sierra had never seen him this scared in his whole six years. It was partly her fault. How could she have been mean? 'Ro-Boy!' she uttered, and was surprised at using his babyhood nickname. He deserved a punishment to learn not to meddle, but she was his *big* sister, wasn't she? And if Rosella could have forgiven Sierra's grandma for such a terrible wrong ... 'I'll get a job, you'll see,' she said, toning her voice down.

She eyed her watch and grimaced at the traffic. Why did everything have to go wrong for her today?

For the second time, the traffic lights changed to red.

Sierra gritted her teeth.

And her mum skidded to a halt. 'A good thing I left the salon when I did,' she said, tapping her fingers on the steering wheel. 'I didn't think of taking time off because I'm rostered for only the mornings on Saturdays. Then today, of all days, Cassie didn't come in. Her mother had slipped and broken her hip, apparently. So we were lumped with her clients' hairdos as well.' The lines on her forehead appeared deeper than at other times. 'I wanted to be there for you, sweetie. Knew this was important to you. Felt like chucking it in, but with Dad's job ...' She went quiet mid-sentence as though she was counting on silence to convey her emotions. 'Of course, I never expected *this*.'

The familiar red brick building came into view.

The Lana Lott Dance Centre.

Sierra gripped her seatbelt, ready to unclip it, wishing she could sprout wings and fly.

'I'll park the car and come in,' her mum said, when they reached the premises.

'Parents aren't allowed into the audition, Mum.'

'Okay, I'll take Rory home and be back to wait for you.' She drove to the entrance.

Sierra leapt out of the car.

∞

Sierra hammered down the now empty passage and into the deserted changing room. She had *three* minutes to get her leotard and tights on without wrinkles, put on her ballet shoes, and tuck her short hairs under her headband to satisfy Miss Lana's uniform code so that she didn't get disqualified before she started.

And then get to the studio.

How on earth had she imagined she could race home and back? It was near impossible even after being driven one way. *Her wonky maths!* Sierra wrestled to keep her head screwed to her neck while she dressed. She didn't dare to check the time any more.

Then she charged along the passage again, feeling she was being chased by the clocks in the centre. Didn't they know she'd trip, she'd fall and that wouldn't be all if she knew the time? But when she got up to the noticeboard, the arms of that clock above it grabbed her.

It was 3.07.
She'd missed the audition.

Chapter 20

Sierra's body went limp, but she staggered on. As she turned right at the end of the passage, she lost her footing and narrowly escaped the wall. Was she hallucinating or was that Evan hanging around by the studio?

'Why aren't you in?'

Him! 'I'm late, I'm late. The girls were at –'

'Steady on! Auditions haven't begun.'

'What?' Sierra stalled. 'But Miss La –'

'It's Mr Trotter, he's been delayed,' Evan said. 'His car has packed up.'

'His car? Again?' A burst of energy hurled Sierra out of her rag-doll state. *You're a life saver, Mr Trotter!* She wrenched the handle of the black double-door. It swung open.

She crossed the threshold.

She was at the audition.

'Name?' a voice enquired at her elbow. A girl with a clipboard was regarding her.

'Sierra Seldon.' Sierra couldn't remember ever seeing her. Why was she being handed an audition number when Miss Lana knew them all so well? Er ... but who was the lady Miss Lana was talking to at the judges' table at the front of the studio? In fact, there were two people. She tried to place them. They appeared vaguely familiar – from the faculty, perhaps? They sat poised with notepads and pens. It was as if Miss Lana had set the event to give her students an auditioning experience.

Sierra pinned on her number with a feeling of apprehension in her stomach. She'd believed it was going to be only Miss Lana. Now she had to face the scrutiny of three pairs of eyes. Why did Miss Lana have to string on the pressure?

Her head down, she tiptoed to join the rest at the far end of the studio, alongside the *barre*.

'Pssst!'

Sierra glanced quickly around her. It was Min sticking her head from the crowd. She pointed her chin at the studio clock and then clapped her hand over her heart. Her eyes were saying, *I was worried sick*.

Thanks, Sierra mouthed, also not wanting to risk talking inside the studio.

The door flew open and Mr Trotter dashed in, dabbing his podgy face with a large hanky. He made for the piano with an apologetic wave at the judges.

Time was closing in on her. How was she going to get into audition mode? Her ballet limbs were in knots after nearly not making it.

Sierra touched her cheek. Was that a cool breeze? Without an open window, she didn't know where it came from, but it seemed to be nudging her to strip what had happened from her mind because it didn't belong to this moment. Hadn't her grandma suffered by clinging to her past? Hadn't Rosella coped better by letting hers go? Why couldn't *she*?

Sierra took a deep breath and emptied her mind.

Then it was on with the audition.

They all did exercises at the centre of the studio at first. Next, a junior teacher demonstrated a sequence. With her nerves in check, Sierra absorbed the slow moves by marking them with her arms and feet. Then they had to perform the combination, one by one. With another big breath, she took her turn.

The sequences that followed tested everything they'd learned. And now Sierra's steps were flowing, naturally, easily ... reaching a better-than-ever-before momentum.

Finally it was acting through dance. Paying attention to how the teacher conveyed emotion through her face and movements, Sierra went on dancing smoothly, effortlessly ...

'The curtain falls,' she murmured, leaving the studio.

She could still hear the music that had told her body and feet what to do. It was as if that music had come from inside her. Funny, though, she hadn't thought about why she was dancing, or even what the outcome might be. Kim? The judges? Was that the reason she forgot them?

How could distractions sneak into her mind when it had been crammed with her dancing? Yup.

She'd been in the moment with her dancing.

Rosella had a point; maybe the thing *was* to be switched-on to the present. Hadn't it at least got her through the audition?

Out of audition mode, Sierra let the burning questions tumble into her mind. How did the judges assess her technique? Had it been up to scratch? She went over what she could recall. Oh, had she wobbled in the *attitude* position just that little bit? With the jumps, her worry was her *sissonne*: had she focussed on her journal entry, 'Think *scissors*'? And were her sequences correct? Then her acting? Being a character? How well had she stacked all that into her performance?

How well had the others?

In reply, Kim bobbed up beside her, brimming with smiles. 'It was great, right? Those sequences were real cool.'

Sierra felt a pang in her heart. Kim would have got perfect scores. Had *she*? Without the applause of an audience as at a concert, she couldn't tell.

She couldn't find out either, until Miss Lana released the cast list.

Chapter 21

The following Saturday afternoon, Sierra got her mum to drop her at the dance centre but paused by the front door, her insides in a twist. She almost didn't want to go in.

This was it, the last ballet class for the term – and the all-important results of the audition. *Go on*, she ordered herself. *Get it over with.*

She could hear the excited hum coming from around the noticeboard, punctuated by squeals and groans. Nobody was even pretending they didn't care about the casting. At least, it wasn't just her.

She wriggled to the front of the group, her eyes going straight to the first entry on the cast list.

Princess Aurora

Show 1: Kim Hasler

Her heart skipped a beat. Kim.

Kim had got it.

Her eyes moved down to the next entry.

Show 2: Kim Hasler

Now her heart froze. Still, Kim. Please, pleeeeeease … She struggled to shift her gaze to the line below.

Show 3: Sierra Seldon

Sierra pressed her palms against her heated cheeks, her emotions in a tangle. She should be glad that she had been given the third show; it was a vote of confidence. The other girls who had tried out would kill for that opportunity.

But it wasn't enough. It wasn't enough for her, and it wouldn't be enough for her mum. To convince her mum, she had to be the *best*. Sort of irreplaceable … sort of … She didn't know what, any more. And with

Kim the star in two shows, she'd be the one dancing her way to the nationals.

Sierra supressed the gamut of sobs rising in her throat; she couldn't cry in front of everyone. They'd smirk. Well, some of them would. They'd laugh. They'd dub her a bad loser and make snide comments. To stop the tears, she batted her eyelids vehemently until a hand landed on her shoulder from behind and made her jump.

It was Min. 'Hap-hap-happy! Meet the Diamond Fairy,' she said, tapping her chest and grinning from ear to ear as though she was stretching it to put on Sierra's face too. 'Off with the scowl. You got the biggie! Aren't you rapt?'

'Except that Kim's doing two shows,' Sierra said, pitching for a not-so-bothered tone, having dumbly allowed her face to reveal her disappointment. She couldn't let the others suss out what this really meant to her; she had to act as if it didn't matter.

'Are you blind?' Min pointed at the note pinned below the cast list.

Entrant for the Junior Showcase National Ballet Competition: Sierra Seldon

How could this be right? Kim was the one starring twice. But ... but ... but, but, this was clearly *her* name. '*Yes!*' Sierra flung her head back and her arms up. Then she high-fived with Min and read the line over and over as if she was saving it in her memory in case the judges forgot their decision.

When at last she detached herself from the board, she turned and bumped into Kim.

'Good on you,' Kim said. Her eyes were friendly and so was her voice.

Well. Wow. Where was her sugary talk? *The love-ballet thing, the love-ballet thing!* Hadn't Kim called her a swell dancer before? Sierra dropped her guard and shot her a smile. 'Thanks. You did pretty well, yourself.'

Kim giggled. 'What do you think of Evan as Prince Florimund? Cool, right?'

'Oh, did he make it?' Sierra asked, pushing hard to sound disinterested, though she had to dig deep to bury the niggly thought of Kim getting double-time with him.

Then she saw Miss Lana flitting up the passage and bounded to her. 'Thank you, Miss Lana!'

Miss Lana's arrival got the others flocking around them.

'*You* did it, Sierra.' Miss Lana's face lit up. 'It's not just your technique. You dance with your heart, feeling the music. That's what makes you stand out.'

Passion, Sierra said silently, recalling Rosella's comment, while she marked a sequence of glory in her head. *If only her mum could hear!*

'It's going to be hard work practising for the concert as well as the competition,' Miss Lana went on. 'Therefore I decided you do Princess Aurora for one show – that way, you'll have fewer rehearsals for it.'

'Thank you, Miss Lana,' Sierra repeated, unable to offer anything new in terms of conversation because now that it was evident why she had been given one show, her mind was engaged in summing up the adjudication as though she was the judge.

And her heart did a victory dance.

She *was* the best.

Miss Lana's hawkish eyes preyed on the others. 'Here at the dance centre we take pride in providing a strong foundation especially for those who intend to go on and train to become professional dancers.' She hawked back to Sierra. 'You seem to be heading in that direction. Is that what you want – a career in dance?'

'My dream!' Sierra said. If only, if only her mum was here.

'You shouldn't have any difficulty getting into a full-time program. We can work on that. Schools and the ever exciting auditions.'

Her goal, exactly, and Miss Lana believed in her! Then reality smacked Sierra on the head, making her writhe. What if she had to quit ballet after the concert? After all this, Miss Lana might even be furious that Sierra had auditioned. Furious.

Miss Lana beamed over Sierra's shoulder. 'She's a talented dancer. You must be proud of her, Mrs Seldon –'

'Mum?' Sierra swivelled to find her mum standing behind her, clutching the dance bag Sierra had forgotten to take from the car. She hadn't noticed her mum joining them because she'd been revelling in Miss Lana's each word.

And Miss Lana had more.

'Sierra could very well get to the final round and do us proud at the nationals,' she said. 'I know she will also delight us as Princess Aurora. She can handle both.'

Sierra sneaked a glance at her mum. She was nodding, and the corners of her mouth were making a smile. Was she being polite? Or, or ... Sierra's heart now staged a dance of hope. She hadn't expected her mum to hear first-hand what the *expert* had to say. What a bonus. Oh, her three-step plan, her precious three-step plan. Could it mean ...

Miss Lana ventured further, gesturing at Sierra. 'Training as a dancer and joining a ballet company could lead to performing on the world stage.'

Sierra glowed, and while Miss Lana talked to the other students, she let her mind take flight, dancing on every continent, even in distant places that had never seen ballet.

Again, she glimpsed at her mum.

Her mum's lips were slightly parted and her eyes were piled with layers of thought.

What was she thinking?

What would she say?

Freaking out, Sierra turned back to Miss Lana, hoping she'd top up her awesome remarks in case Sierra's mum was not yet hooked. But Miss Lana was leaving.

It was time to take the ultimate plunge.

Sierra looked her mum in the eye.

And it was like watching her mum hand her the bouquet reserved for the prima ballerina. If that wasn't a *yes* for ballet, what was?

'Oh, Mum,' she said.

Her mum extended her arms and Sierra walked right into them.

'Ignoring your passion is not going to quell it. Why didn't I see that?' Her mum's eyes were teary. 'We will make it work,' she whispered.

We? Sierra basked in the warmth that filled her heart. That little word encapsulated all the support she had longed for. It was like having the largest cheering squad. She gulped at her mum's courage to make that pledge to her despite her dad's job going and everything. How could she have wished she was Kim?

After her class, she phoned Rosella.

'The star in one show and the entrant for the national competition!' she announced, as soon as Rosella picked up.

'*You made it!* I knew you could.' Rosella's voice danced down the line. 'And your mum?'

'You should have seen the *yes* in her eyes!' Sierra chuckled. 'Now I can become a ballerina and live my dream. What can be neater than that?'

Thank you for buying this book

If you enjoyed reading *The Secret of the Ballet Book*, please be so kind as to let others know about it by leaving a review wherever you bought the book.

Thank you in advance. Your support is truly appreciated.

Best wishes,
Navita Dello

67072665R00070

Made in the USA
Lexington, KY
31 August 2017